ISBN: 9798533841436

Warning

This is a dark romance meaning there are themes commonly
found in dark romance, this includes a captor/captive
romance, kidnap, murder, violence, drug & alcohol use,
heavy sexual content & strong language.
It is advised not to be read by those under the age of 18.

She kissed me.
She kissed the devil.
Only a beautiful soul like hers would kiss the damned.

- Daniel Saint

LITTLE
Bird

TWISTED CITY DUET
BOOK I

RIA WILDE

Prologue

Lex

"Get down!" The order comes from Ryker, a beast of a man with an even beastlier temper. He drops like a lead weight, his body hitting the floor with a loud thud, and I follow, a little dazed, my ears ringing and pulsing, the blood pumping like a drum inside my head. The blast that happened only moments ago was, to say the least, unexpected.

I feel blood, warm and sticky, slowly trickling down the side of my face, rolling over my skin until it seeps into the stubble lining my jaw. The smell of ash, blood and death saturates the air. Dust makes it almost impossible to see, huge clouds of white smog disturbed only by the wind blowing in through the smashed windows at the front of the house, curling like snakes as it is illuminated from the flood lights outside.

What the fuck is happening!?

On my front, my elbows to the ground, I begin to crawl across the debris, pushing passed the dead bodies and the puddles of crimson blooming in the rubble. Death wasn't a new sight for me and seeing these people, people I know, staring wide eyed at the ceiling with blood leaking from various wounds does nothing to me. It brings no emotion, no pain or guilt or sadness.

Death, after all, was inevitable. One of the only things in life that is guaranteed. I learned long ago that you'd never be able to run from it, you cannot hide but sometimes, and it's rare, you *could* control how it ended.

There was no way, with the life I lead that I would be granted a peaceful exit. You enter this world violently; I see it only fitting that be the way you leave it too. And that's how I hoped it would be. I wanted bloody, destructive, a ruin that flattens buildings and is remembered for years to come. But that time is yet to arrive, this won't be the end for me.

I grip my gun, pulling it from where I had stashed it earlier this evening and move towards the smashed windows. The device had been launched through the glass where it landed and promptly exploded. There was no warning, no tell, one moment we were enjoying a small gathering with some of the city officials, an event set up by my father, the next, the window shattered, and a small round object hit the mahogany floor, a little red light flashing rapidly. It must have only been a few seconds at most and then *boom*! The device detonated, sending bodies flying. Some were hit with shrapnel, others slammed into the walls or other objects close by.

"Alexander!" I hear Ryker call out, but it's muffled, like I'm listening whilst I'm under water. "Lex!"

The man was only doing his job, protecting me but at the end of the day, he may be a beast, a monster to anyone looking in from the outside, but I was the motherfucking devil. And the devil wouldn't take this shit laying down. No fucking way would that shit fly, he'll be standing amongst the carnage with a smile on his face.

Whoever had just hit us has broken the one rule that separates us men from beasts.

There's no hiding the fact that, as the Silver family, we had made countless enemies, but in that list of foes, who would be stupid enough to hit us like this?

No one is innocent, they never have been but there are unwritten laws that are woven into the fabric of who we are. We run this city and have done for generations, those around us abide by it if they want to remain within the city limits and capitalizing on what we have created.

With my Glock gripped in my hands, slicked with blood, I rise to survey the gardens through the broken window. The flood lights are blaring white light onto the lawns outside the house in the centre of the city and I can see shapes moving through the grounds.

It's a fucking small army.

"Who the fuck is it?" I demand.

"The Valentine's!" Ryker answers immediately.

The fucking Valentine's.

I growl but don't respond as I watch the small band of armed men approach. Of course it's the fucking

Valentine's.

Those sick motherfuckers had been threatening us since their last shipment got intercepted. If they had listened to the fucking instructions, we wouldn't have gotten involved, but clearly they were too dumb to catch on.

The Silver's rule Brookeshill and whilst it's big, there's no room for the two of us, not when Valentine wants to take the crown.

"Lex!" My father's voice rings through the chaos, through the shadows and bloodshed, I hear the grief tearing him apart. My heart sinks, my gut churns. I don't feel the physical pain of my injuries, years of conditioning and training makes that a dull ache in the background, but this, this is something I haven't been trained for.

I may be ruthless. Brutal. The fucking King but no amount of warning or preparation would have made me ready for what I see walking through the ruin towards me.

My father, battered, dirty, bleeding, carrying a lifeless body in his arms. Her hair dangles limply, her arms and legs swinging with each step he takes towards my prone body at the window.

"Mr Silver," Ryker panics, "Mr Silver, they're preparing to fire, you need to get down!"

The men take aim out the windows, if I look both left and right, I could see them all, hidden for the event but now available and ready to be used.

The Silver's are royalty in this city. We are Kings.

Queens. Fucking Gods. And these guys, the ones preparing to rage war on the intruders are loyal and they always would be.

My father doesn't heed Ryker's warning, instead his legs numbly carry him forward, towards me.

"Cover me," I demand from Ryker who immediately takes my position. The fucker is huge and takes up the entire window, using his mass to shield me as I move towards my father.

As feared, the woman in his arms is dead. Her eyes are open, her smooth skin covered in blood, the white dress no longer white and instead stained in crimson and black.

I hold it back. The emotion that begs to be released gets lodged in the back of my throat becoming acidic and poisonous. It makes my windpipe close, my lungs constrict.

"Son," my father's voice cracks.

We're talking about a man who never questions his morals when he raises the barrel of a gun to someone's head, never bats an eyelid when the blade of his knife slices across someone's throat and will stand upon his enemies with his chin lifted and madness in his eyes, breaking – fucking *breaking* – in front of his men.

We don't do that.

We don't show weakness.

"I'll kill them all," I declare. "Slowly. Painfully. If it's war the Valentine's want, then it's war I'll give them."

5

1

Wren

Six months later

"Again," Griff orders, breathing in heavily with his body still prone to fight, watching from his position in the middle of the mat.

The rims of my nostrils flare, my skin wet with sweat and probably a little bit of blood too. The motherfucker got in a cheap shot earlier and it's been bleeding a steady stream ever since, a stream which mingles with my perspiration to make it watery enough to drip from my chin and onto the blue foam beneath my bare feet.

I grunt and cross the mat in a sprint, my legs carrying me stealthily. When I'm close, instead of running right into the guy like he expects, I leap to the side, spinning around and hooking my arm around his throat, throwing my body down. I quickly release and land in a crouch to the side as Griff hits the mat hard. His back thuds and his head bounces, and for a moment, just a brief second, I worry I went in too hard.

Unexpectedly, a rough laugh vibrates from his chest, "Good. That was good."

"Are we done?" I breathe in deep, trying to steady the chaotic thump of my heart. I wipe the blood with the back of my hand, no doubt spreading it over my cheek but at this point, I don't care. I have places to be, people to see.

"Yeah, Wren, we're done." Griff levels himself up onto his elbows, quirking one dark brow my way, "You're distracted today." I liked Griff, I've been training with him for a couple of years now and he's taught me everything I know but because of that, he knew me well enough to be able to pick up when my head wasn't in the session.

"I'm busy," I snap back, grabbing my towel and rubbing it across my brow and then down my face before swiping up my water bottle and taking a couple of healthy gulps.

"Too busy for your family?"

And there it is. Regardless of whether I liked Griff, I knew any and all information he got from me during these sessions would end up back with my father. He had become a middle man, a messenger of sorts.

I roll my eyes, "More like they're too busy for me."

"Your father asked me to request your presence at dinner tonight."

"Of course he did," it's like the man has a link to my diary – if I had one of course – and purposely steps in when he thinks I'm about to go out and have fun. God forbid I do anything where I actually enjoy myself. "Tell him no."

"We all know, 'no', isn't in the vocabulary that your father understands."

"Well give him a dictionary at the same time, you can find it under the letter N."

Griff chuckles, "I'll tell him, but I'd turn your phone off if I were you, you'll have a thousand voicemails by morning."

I nod. That would be likely, "Later Griff, take some aspirin for the headache."

He shakes his head and climbs up from the mat as I push through the doors that'll take me back to the changing rooms. The gym is quiet this evening, only a few other people work out on the equipment in the main room, the steady thump of sneakers on the treadmill mingling with the heavy bass music that crackles from a sound system that has seen better days.

Whenever we train, we use one of the back rooms, a private area that's usually reserved for lessons, but Griff owns the gym himself and personally sees to my training. Training my father demands I take, along with the gun training, knife training and any other means of self-defense. The man is paranoid, that much is obvious.

I supposed I had him to thank for the ease in which I'm able to defend and protect myself, in this day and age, being a woman who can hold her own is everything. I shower quickly and then change into the dress I had stashed in the bag, pulling out my makeup and hair brush at the same time. It wasn't ideal having to hit the bar straight from training, but with time against me, I had no choice.

I knew better than to believe my dad was simply just paranoid. I'd heard the late-night calls and witnessed the guys coming and going in hours not meant to be seen by civilization. Not guys like him, dressed in tailored suits and Italian loathers, but big guys, in leather and ripped jeans. It wasn't their clothes that set them apart from the men my dad usually associates with, but the ruthless glint they all held in their eyes. Not much scared me but those fuckers were *terrifying*.

Now you tell me, what would a man, who sits as a CEO of a million-dollar company, have that meant he dealt with guys who carry guns tucked into the waistbands of their jeans and concealed blades beneath their trouser legs.

It's not the behavior of a man who lives life within the carefully set boundaries.

The conversations I've overheard suggest something much darker, dirtier in fact, drugs, guns…

I had no doubt my father was involved in something way bigger than the company he is determined to give to me when he retires. Something much seedier and dangerous.

The paranoia is one reason he forces me to train like this but it's his lifestyle that has determined that fact and made it a necessity.

I apply a small layer of makeup to my face, hiding the flush in my cheeks still present from training, trying my best to conceal the split in my lip, and run my fingers through my still wet hair, the strands curling already. By the end of the night it'll be wild, the curls tight and unruly, but I don't have time to tend to it now.

Rory – Aurora, my best friend – was meeting me in twenty minutes at a cocktail bar down the street and if I were late, she'd have my head. We made sure to plan far in advance, like six weeks in advance and she's been reminding me every other day for the past three weeks. My schedule was always manic, thanks to my family but I made sure my father knew and understood tonight was blocked out. His request I join him for dinner isn't his want for a nice family meal, it is, in fact, a try at controlling my life, just like it always is.

The dress clings to my frame, the neckline low, dipping well below my cleavage, almost to my naval and the hem sits just above my knee, the swirls of black ink on my thigh only just peeking out from the bottom. It's late summer so the nights are still warm enough to forego a jacket which means my sleeve tattoo is on full show tonight. I stare at my reflection, at the copper hair already kinking and curling atop my head and my wide green eyes that seem almost too big for my face.

It'll do, I guess. My feet slip into the black strappy sandals I had packed to go with the dress and then I walk from the locker rooms and out into the evening. The light of day clings to the skyline, the sky a dusty indigo colour with slashes of pink and orange. My Audi lights blink when I press the button and then I climb into the drivers seat, shoving my gym bag into the back where it'll likely stay for a week. Music blasts from the stereo

10

when I turn the key in the ignition and press on the gas, peeling out of the near empty lot of the gym, heading towards the bar. It's where we're starting but not where we're finishing according to Aurora. It's been far too long since I hit the clubs with my best friend, after the last time it had become almost impossible to plan anything with her, until I put my foot down with my father.

I was twenty-three, far too young to spend every weekend locked up in the apartment I rented downtown, but with the security personnel my father hired it had become impossible to escape.

I had managed, somehow, to convince my dad to let it go. What happened a few months back was something that could have happened to anyone. The guys that cornered me after a night out were thugs, criminals and whilst I had tried to handle them myself, I still ended up in the hospital with several broken ribs and a face that looked like I had gone ten rounds in the ring with a professional MMA fighter. I took out at least three of them, a point my dad overlooks. Ever since then he's hired bodyguards to see me everywhere. Not tonight though. Tonight I'm free.

A little bubble of excitement works its way through my system, and I press on the gas, heading down the street to my apartment building where I'm planning on leaving my car. I park in the underground garage and then take the elevator up to street level. There are still enough people and traffic out that I don't have to worry about being in trouble and wander down the sidewalk towards the glowing blue sign for the cocktail bar I was meeting Rory at.

I find her perched at a high-top table, her black dress tight and revealing, her blonde hair dead straight and hanging around her face like a curtain. She's not like me in the sense of the word, where I grew up in a huge mansion at the edge of the city, she grew up down at the trailer park with an alcoholic father and a mother who walked out on her when she was only three.

Not that you would know it by looking at her now. She was finishing up college and will go on to become a teacher at Brookeshill elementary school.

She waves enthusiastically and I cross the room, the clip of my heels loud in the quiet space. The music is on low, a gentle hum rather than blasting, and groups of people laugh and converse all around me.

Fuck, I hadn't realized how long it had been since I felt normal.

I try to ignore all the shit with my family, the dodgy dealings, the late-night phone calls and the odd blood stains on my father's sleeves but that shit isn't easy to forget. I know, *I know*, that my family is far from clean, I just hope he didn't expect me to follow in his footsteps.

I had no idea what exactly he was involved in, and I don't want to know.

"Damn," Rory grins, "you look great."

I flick my hair and flutter my lashes dramatically, with a laugh I say, "Thanks."

With her manicured fingers, she pushes the pornstar martini towards me and takes a sip of her own, "To freedom!"

I chuckle, tipping my head back, "To freedom!"

The first sip of the cocktail goes down far too smoothly, "So where to after this?"

She wiggles her brow, "Club Silver."

I quirk a brow, "Wow, how'd you secure that?"

Club Silver opened in downtown a little over four months ago and has been in popular demand ever since. The city was alive at night, with hundreds of clubs thriving, but since that one opened, it's where everyone wants to go, to the point you now have to book in advance and pay a premium booking fee to secure a space.

She purses her lips with a frown, "I'm not really sure, actually," she laughs, "I ran into some guy the other day, a bit scary looking but he was handing out personal invites to the club and I just so happened to be in the right place at the right time."

I shrug, "Seems like fate to me."

Rory giggles and tips back the remaining dregs of her cocktail before she hops from the stool and heads to the bar to order a few more. I sit there, the alcohol I've consumed warming my veins, settling into my empty stomach. Shit I didn't have time to eat after training and by the end of the night I'm sure I'll be feeling it. I glance towards the front of the bar, looking behind the servers running back and forth to accompany the heaving crowd to see if they do food or even small appetizers, just to line my stomach and yet what I find, is anything but food.

Well I mean, I suppose he could be classed as a snack, I guess.

A tailored suit, the fit not too tight yet tight enough to tease at the muscles he has concealed underneath. The white shirt is tucked into black pants, the buckle of his belt gleaming in the dim lighting. Silver cufflinks, no tie, the top two buttons undone to reveal tanned, olive toned skin. Dark stubble lines the sharp edge of his jaw, high, defined cheek bones and low set brows, low enough to cast shadows over his steel eyes. A mop of dark hair falls over his forehead, too long to be deemed professional and I should know having been around the stuffy suits working at my father's offices every day, none of them would dare let their hair grow that long. Always short, always tamed, like the good little robots they are.

He's staring right at me. I've never been one to flirt or even hook up, I'm no virgin but the look he's levelling me with can only be classed as *hot*.

Though it's not quite there, like something is missing but I just can't figure out what.

Sure, from the way his eyes travel over my body, his gaze moving over my bare legs, stopping a little at the black ink peeking out from the hem of my dress but then moving on quickly over my hips, to the curve of my waist and then further up, following the deep V of my dress where my breasts push together – thank you body tape – and then down my right arm where the ink is etched into my skin. Flowers and mandalas, intricate and delicate, feminine, though my family hate them. It's probably why I did it. I knew they wouldn't like the art, just like the nose ring, just like the piercing in my naval.

I was young when I did them, a little naïve and yet I don't regret it at all.

A frown mars his brow, as if confused but it happens so quickly I wonder if I imagined it and then his eyes travel the rest of the way up my body, over my collar and neck before finally levelling his stare with my own.

He tips a short crystal glass to his lips, a small amount of amber liquid pouring into his mouth, keeping his eyes on me over the rim of the glass.

When I finally allow myself to concentrate my eyes on his and truly look, all I find is heat, an intense burn but it's mingled with a ruthlessness I'm sad to recognize. A coldness, a brutality I've seen in the guys that visit my father. His is harder, deeper, colder, like that side of him isn't something that comes out every now and then, it is what makes him the man he is. A shiver runs its way down my spine, a warning signal and natural survival instinct to let me know I'm in the company of a predator.

My father made damn sure I'd never be a damsel, even the attack a few months back I stood my ground, but I can't help feeling less than and weaker here. He isn't the type of guy I'd want to encounter in the dark. Though you'll be damn sure I'd give it a good go.

There are monsters everywhere, Wren, my fathers voice echoes inside my head, a phantom whisper ensuring I stay alert at all times, *it isn't the monster under your bed or in your closet that you need to watch out for, it's the ones that look like me and you that you should fear. It's the ones that seem completely normal and yet they hide an evil in their eyes. That's where you'll find it, Wren, in their eyes. When you see that, make sure you run. Run as far and as fast as you can.*

I didn't want to run though. I wanted to show the world I could handle myself. I didn't need bodyguards and security. My father saw it fit to train me to the absolute best of my ability, he honed my skill, taught me how to use my size and speed to my advantage, all because of his shady side business and whilst I may *disagree* with it, I wanted to prove I could handle myself.

I square my shoulders and narrow my eyes, a pretty face and a body made of sin wouldn't be enough to deceive me. He can believe he's found an easy target in me, but I'm prepared to prove him wrong.

Aurora saunters back with two glasses filled with a sparkling pink liquid laced with small pieces of cut strawberries and hops up onto the stool. Her brows draw down as she follows my eyes and slides my drink towards me.

"Well hello tall, dark, and handsome," Rory sucks her teeth.

I force my eyes away and turn back to my friend, giving the guy my back which seems like a mistake. You never turn your back on a predator. I'm not prey though and if he chooses to strike, I'll be ready.

"What's this?" I ask, sliding my glass the final few inches towards me and wrap my lips around the straw, drawing from the glass.

Fizz and sugar hit my tongue, the drink is so sweet it makes my jaw ache. Rory just shrugs, "Last one and then we're heading to Silver."

I nod, taking another sip. The alcohol buzz from earlier has dissipated, leaving only awareness in its wake. I'm alert, ready, my senses homing in on my surroundings, listening for approaching footsteps. If there is one thing I have learned from all the self defense classes I have partaken in, it's that the human instinct to danger is very rarely wrong, but as humans evolved we started to ignore that basic nature, choosing to blindly trust and naively believe we were all safe.

We drink our drinks and I act my part, laughing, talking, joking and it's only when I'm halfway to finished, that the heat in my back finally subsides. I subtly glance behind me to find the stool at the bar vacant, the space where he was occupying completely empty.

I relax. Hopefully, he's gone on to find some other helpless girl to terrorize.

I don't know who he is, or what he could ever want with a girl like me but I sensed that danger and when I saw him, the man with eyes so pale they rivaled the moon, I could tell that his breed of brutality wasn't one I'd easily survive.

2

Lex

I've studied the images. I've followed the lines of her bountiful curves, the dips and flares of her thighs, her hips. I've watched videos. I've witnessed her beauty through those, seen it already with my own two eyes, and even then, I thought she was a beautiful woman, but seeing her here, in a dress that barely covers her sinfully delectable body, with her delicately painted tattoos and wild red hair, I was caught off guard, unprepared for what she could look like face to face.

The legs, the body, the face with the mass of copper curls and the innocent eyes.

The innocent eyes. No one is innocent, there is always something they are guilty for, we are all sinners here but there's something about the way the innocence looks on her that almost makes me feel guilty.

Almost.

I laugh at myself. Emotion. I lost that a long time ago. The guilt tugs at the corners of my mind, trying to push in but I shut that shit out. Just like I was taught. The girl is a means to an end. The need for vengeance far outweighs a crisis of conscience. I am not a man of morality, and it wasn't physically possible for a woman like her to suddenly arouse any sense of right and wrong. We didn't get to be where we were with integrity or decency.

She's gorgeous, I can appreciate that, but in this walk of life I encounter beautiful women all the time, I have them on my arm, in my bed, impaled on my cock and screaming my name. There was nothing special about her apart from the purpose in which I needed her for.

I glance down at my phone, looking at the image on the screen.

Wren.

Twenty-three, recent graduate with honors.

Smart girl.

And *exactly* who it is I need.

The plan has been in the works for six months now, and we're finally in the last stretch.

My father hasn't been the same since the night my mother was murdered, and it's been on me to keep going. I stepped up. It's *my* fucking time and I'm going to start it by sending a message.

A message to show no mercy, no pity. There will be no question from here on out who rules this city. I am King.

And they're all going to fucking know it.

I push off the stool, my eyes still trained on her back, following the curve of her waist, the flare of her hips, the swell of her ass and allow myself, just for a moment, to picture how her plump lips would look wrapped around my dick. It's a shame such potential will end up buried in a six foot ditch.

Marcus Valentine was smart, I'd give him that, *if* I could give him anything.

I knew exactly where she would end up tonight, after all, it was my plan this entire time, and there was no way I was letting her slip from my fingers.

Leaving her in the cocktail bar with her friend, I head down the street to Club Silver. Music thumps from the building, filling the street in both directions and I head right for the front doors, slipping in past Matthew who nods at me and continues checking ID's at the door.

The dim lighting of the club casts me in shadows and instead of weaving the crowd that grinds and gyrates to the nineties music that blasts from the speakers I cut left and head through a door, camouflaged to look like it's part of the wall, one that is marked Storage but drops to a steep stairwell that will take me beneath the club. There were only two doors that will get me down here, this one and a second one outside. The concrete is thick, the music above only a steady thump as I descend, vibrating the walls.

A second club opens up before me, one not known to the people above, to the simple mundane citizens of this city, one where deals go ahead, gambling, girls in scantily clad gear that rub up against men in suits with lines of coke dusting the tables and offered on silver platters. A place where blood is as common as the soil lining a flower bed and corruption is what fills the pockets of this city's most influential people.

A girl wearing red lace lingerie struts towards me, her skin almost glowing beneath the lighting, a smirk lifting the corners of her red painted mouth as she offers out a tray. Right alongside the scotch are two lines of the white shit and I debate, I really do, but with the need to have my head in the plan I bypass it for this evening.

I take a glass and throw it back, draining the amber liquid inside before taking the second and leaving the drugs.

"Anything else?" She asks in a low sultry voice, her eyes hooded, the long lashes she's applied casting shadows over her cheeks. She thrusts her chest out, the half-moons of her breasts spilling out of the cups that hold the rest of her in. "Does the boss need a little relaxation perhaps?"

I couldn't have any distractions tonight, I wasn't risking my plan.

"Another time," I tell her, leaning in to whisper the words in her ear, "make sure to find me when I'm next here."

"Yes sir," she breathes and I step back, eyeing the athletically toned body, slim, long legs and narrow hips.

"What's your name?" I ask.

"Josie," she answers.

"Have a good night, Josie," I say, extracting a wad of cash from my pocket and tucking it into the waist band of her tight, red lace panties.

A flush of pink rises to her cheeks, even under this dim light I see it, but I leave her still and head towards the elevators on the other side that'll take me up to the balcony that overlooks the revelers in the club.

My key card opens the door and muffled noise greets me inside the metal cart. A mixture of the low, erotic music of the underground club and the heavy bass of Club Silver above. The elevator is slow, but I don't mind as it takes me back up.

In the time it takes to move up levels, I remember the faces I saw, the Mayor and police chief were here tonight, that's good, buried in the lines of coke offered to them and the girls perched in their laps. The hidden cameras will be enough should they ever step out of line. A couple of high-ranking corporate bodies were there too, a few government officials.

Of course these people would never enter through the main doors, they would slip in behind, down a back alley that would take them through the back entrance and then further down to the club below. Club Silver offered them anonymity, something they'd never get anywhere else. Everyone had a darkness to them though they were never given the opportunity for it to come out. That's where I come in. I give them what they crave and in return, I get what I need.

When I set up the club this was exactly what I had in mind.

My father was a ruthless leader, but he didn't have it all

planned out.

He went forward on brutality and bloodshed, fear that would stop even the fiercest of men, but I would be smarter. I will *stay* king, because of my reputation people knew, like a deep-rooted instinct that in this city, they were the prey and me, I was the predator. I didn't fear that these men would cross me and even if they did, I had plenty of back up to ensure they stayed in line. Images. Transactions. Videos. All of which could be shared to the entire city, to the entire world in fact in a matter of seconds. It is that knowledge that keeps them in my pocket and me on top.

Blackmail.

Every man in this city was riding on power and if you threatened to take that away you could guarantee they'd be on their knees begging. Every damn time.

It makes life a whole lot easier when the cops aren't breathing down your neck and the mayor is backing your every move without a single question.

And if that didn't work, well there are other methods of keeping people quiet and in line. Something a lot bloodier. There wasn't much I wouldn't do, blood to me was as normal as turning on a tap. A little messier but a whole lot more fun.

The elevator doors slide open though now the clock has struck eleven, the music and atmosphere of the club has changed. The playlist is now blasting out more modern music, hip hop, garage, and the bodies on the dance floor continue to grind. There is no need to grab a drink, one is waiting for me as I exit the elevator and I lift it from the tray, continuing my way forward until I'm at the glass railing and looking down at the floor below.

Ry steps up beside me, "it's all set, boss."

He'd started calling me boss about a month after my mother's death and coming from my closest and longest friend, it took some getting used to. In closed quarters, we were still that, but here, in the open, he was nothing more than a loyal dog, he knew it, I knew it.

I dip my chin in acknowledgment and sip at the scotch in my hand. Behind me a few guys take the affection a couple of the wait staff give them and for now, I allow it. Until *she* shows, they can do whatever the fuck they want.

They've earned it after all.

It's a little past midnight when a security guard steps into my space, "She's here, Mr Silver," he whispers close to my ear so only I can hear.

I nod and continue to watch.

She's a presence to be known. A goddess amongst the mundane. Her unruly copper hair and tight curves draw attention but it's the look in her eyes that has people stepping away to create a path. Her friend tags along behind, following the tempest that is Wren Valentine.

"Damn," Ryker chuckles.

I risk a glance his way, taking my eyes off her for a second, "What?"

"I mean, Wren is," he presses his fingers to his lips and blows a kiss, "but her friend, I'd drop to my knees and promise her the world if I could."

"You always did like the blondes," I grumble, turning my attention back to the girl in question.

She makes it to the bar and leans forward, no doubt showing the deep cut of her dress to draw attention. She was beautiful and she knew exactly how to use it. I liked a woman unafraid of using her strengths to her advantage, but I also wasn't stupid enough to believe that it was only her body she could use to win over the enemy. Her smarts were impressive and if I were any other man, I may even congratulate her on her achievements. But I am not any other man and that girl, leaning over the bar to get what she wanted, was exactly where I needed her to be because I deemed it so.

It's a matter of moments before she's served and then she's passing back a cocktail of some sort to her friend and a simple drink for herself, a beverage with cola I assume judging from the dark colour of it.

With a grin they weave back through the crowd to the dance floor.

I need information from the girl and yet my mind can't help but snag on the way she moves to the music, the hypnotic way her hips sway and her body curls. She brings her arms up, her hands tucking into the under layers of her hair as she sensually sways to the beat. I'd call it magic if didn't know any better. She was a fucking siren.

"Fuck," I hear a guy say behind me, "I'd fucking destroy that."

I follow his gaze and, low and behold, it's Wren he's talking about.

She is fucking *glorious*.

She'll look even better when she is strapped to a bed, legs spread, curls wild around her face, at mercy to me, the fucking king.

I twist my head to him, my eyes narrowed, jaw tight, "What did you just say?"

His eyes meet mine and he visually cowers, "Nothing," a stutter, "nothing boss."

"Keep your fucking eyes in your head," I tell him, my voice warning enough as I turn back to Wren.

A couple of guys have descended on her and her friend, one has slipped behind her, his hips moving forward to grind into her ass.

Her brows draw low and she spins on him, fists balling. I can't hear what she says but he backs off, raising his hands in surrender.

Wren resumes dancing but it's not long before another guy steps up to try and claim what is rightfully mine.

My nostrils flare.

"Keep your eye out," I tell Ryker.

He nods once, knowing my entire plan as I take the first step down to the dance floor. I feel his gaze follow me until I find my mark in the middle of the dance floor.

Wren smells as good as she looks, sweet and yet deadly, it assaults my senses as I step up close behind her.

She spins on me, her little fists balled up real tight, her

brows pulled down low and violence shining in her eyes.

"You," She accuses.

"Me," I answer back, knowing she already clocked me back at the cocktail bar.

Her eyes narrow but her hands squeeze my biceps absentmindedly, her nails digging in just enough to allow a bite against my skin, "You found me."

I laugh though it holds no humour as I lean in and whisper in her ear, "I own this place. It appears *you* found *me*."

Her breath comes out in a gasp that teases my hair and brushes against the shell of my ear.

"Who are you?"

"You want to know?" I ask.

Her hands slide from my biceps to the lapels of my suit jacket. She seems to be at war with herself, wanting to know more but telling herself she shouldn't. Good, it means the book smart leaches into the street smart. Her eyes narrow further as my arms slip around her waist, holding her flush to my body. Seeing and feeling are two very different things, you can imagine what something may feel like but until it's in your grasp, it will only ever be make believe. Feeling the way her waist dips and curves is so much more than what I could have imagined. The urge, the primal need to simply take her, have her, *own* her almost has me wishing to throw her over my shoulder and lock her up for completely different reasons.

"Yes, I want to know."

"You can call me Alexander. Or Lex."

"Surname?"

"Silver."

I wait and then wait some more for the realization to come but it never hits.

"I'm Wren," she continues, sliding her hands to my shoulders, "Wren Lawson."

"Want to know me a little more, Wren Lawson?"

A grin tugs at her plump mouth, her lips stained with a deep burgundy colour, "I don't think so."

My brows shoot up. Was there ever a day I had been denied?

"No?"

"No."

My fingers trail down the curve of her waist until I find her hip where my fingers then grip, biting into her flesh. Her eyes flash something dark, seductive, dirty but she quickly conceals it all. "Goodnight, Mr Silver."

I let her weave back through the crowd towards the bar, watching her, if she knew who I was she would have bolted for the door. A sheep in the lion's den was a dead fucking sheep and yet here she still is.

Suspicion and curiosity war with each other in my head.

But at the end of the day, this was a war and she was the next step to winning.

3

Lex

Fuck knows why, but I let her continue thinking she's nice and safe here, whilst I question everything from my perch on the balcony.

"She's playing dumb," Ryker shrugs, "perhaps she's here to do the exact same thing you are."

She sways mesmerizingly to the music, her hips moving in that tight little dress. Surely her father wouldn't have sent his precious little girl here. No that man is a lot, and he makes stupid choices, but I know his weakness.

Her. Wren Valentine.

And he wouldn't send her to me if she were of value to him.

She told me her surname was Lawson but that isn't true. Not even a little and even if I didn't know exactly who she was, I'd spot the Valentine looks in her from a mile away.

My molars grind, what the fuck is going on?

Her friend wobbles unsteadily, almost toppling over but Wren grabs her quickly, her reflexes sharp. With a shake of a head and a few words I'll never even hope of catching, she guides her towards the exit.

Shit.

"Move," I order, abruptly standing and heading back to the elevator. We're on the street in less than a few minutes but when I round the corner the girl is nowhere to be seen.

"Fuck."

"Why did you stall?"

I turn my anger to my second hand, my eyes narrowing. "Excuse me?"

Ryker's eyes flick to the men behind me and he realizes quickly how he just fucked up. I don't get questioned. Not here, not at home and especially not in front of my men.

Getting her to the club was the easiest way to lure her into my trap but now she's gone which means it's going to be considerably harder. And bloodier.

I've scouted her apartment, armed guards are on call twenty-four seven, there were probably even a few in the club tonight but with the amount of people in there they never would have seen it. Not that it mattered. I wanted Valentine to know who had the little princess and the few to the many wouldn't have stood a chance.

Cooling the anger, I turn to the two that followed us out,

"Get back inside, Ryker with me."

I head in the opposite direction of the club and cut through a back alley across the street, turning at the end through a door that will lead me down to the underground parking garage. The beep of my Maserati is loud in the silence of the night, echoing off the concrete walls. My shoes tap furiously across the ground.

Ryker is silent behind me and when I get to the car, I throw open the door and slide inside. The entire ride across the city is quiet, the tension making the air in the car tight and coiled, ready to snap.

I don't address the question he asked before because I didn't have the answer. And right now I don't have time to fuck up. I just didn't expect her to up and leave so suddenly. I do not make mistakes but there's always a first for everything. Her apartment building is dark, all but one. The lights inside are on, lighting up the windows like a damn Christmas tree in the darkness.

"How many?"

"Five," Ryker answers, "Probably two inside."

I nod, reaching into my jacket to check my ammo. Ryker does the same.

"You sure you want to do this?" Ryker asks, "We can send a couple of the guys. It'll be just as effective."

"We leave one alive, I want him to send a message."

Ryker nods.

There was a limited window in which we could take this opportunity so whilst the guard, trying to pretend to be a normal citizen wandering the streets at night, is turned, I climb silently from the car, heading in that direction.

I hear two distinctive pops immediately, not as loud as they should be thanks to the silencer on the gun as Ryker takes out the two guards posted on the other side of the street.

I level my Glock, take aim, and pull the trigger.

The bullet hits my target in the back of the skull, splattering blood up the wall. He hits the ground with a thud, a puddle of crimson pooling around his head.

I swipe a card at the door and head inside, pausing to listen for footsteps.

Just when I think they aren't coming, heavy boots hit the stairs to my left. I press against the wall, my body hidden from view until I see the legs of the first guard. I shoot out his knee and he tumbles down the remaining steps, hitting the floor with a grunt. Before he can even look at my face, I put a bullet between his eyes and take the stairs up two at a time. I find Ryker in the hall, his arm cuffed around the last guard's neck in a choke hold. The man thrashes for a final time but then goes out like a light.

Ryker just simply drops him, raising his hand to wipe a trickle of blood from his face. "Fucker got in a cheap shot." He grumbles, kicking the guy.

I roll my eyes and head to the door. She's still awake inside so as soon as I boot this door down, she'll likely scream and bolt, so I need to be prepared.

I count in my head, lift my foot and hit the door right at

the weak spot. It flies open and slams into the wall with a loud crash, causing ornaments and picture frames to fall from their shelves and shatter against the floor.

When I step inside, gun levelled in front of me I almost laugh at the scene waiting for me.

Wren stands on the other side of her living room, her own gun pointed right at my head. Ryker steps in behind me, his own weapon aimed at her. We've got ourselves a good old-fashioned stand-off.

"I can take you out before he shoots me," she threatens, jerking her chin towards Ryker. There's no fear in her voice, no tremble or worry.

Hmm, that's interesting.

"How good is your aim?" I ask, cocking my head, "because if you're going to shoot me, you're going to want to make sure it kills me."

"Oh it'll kill you," her lips curl back, showing her white teeth, "What do you want?"

The fact that she hasn't shot me already is telling enough, all bark, no bite. Not like me, my bark is just as vicious as my bite.

"Put the gun down," Ryker snarls, "put it down!"

"Get the fuck out!" She screams back.

Girl's got balls.

Ryker takes a menacing step forward and she moves her aim away from me, levelling it on Ryker. There's still no fear though. She's calculating her escape. Her eyes dart between the two of us and then to the exit behind us, it's done so quickly I'm sure she thinks I haven't seen it. But I see everything.

I allow myself a look at her for the first time since finding a gun pointed at my head. She's in sleep shorts, tiny cotton ones and a tank that reveals a slither of pale skin around her hips. Her copper hair is pulled into a pony tail and she doesn't have an ounce of makeup on her face. Her green eyes narrow and her jaw clamps tight. I can appreciate beauty and this girl has it in spades. It always was the psychotic ones that got me off the most.

"What did my father do?" She suddenly asks, "Does he owe you money or something?"

I laugh, "Oh he owes me something. And I'm here to take payment."

"The cash is in the safe," she tells me.

I lick my teeth, shaking my head, "Do I look like I need your money?"

Her brows twitch as if she wants to frown but she is good at hiding most of her emotions.

We're at a stand-off right now and time is ticking. I have no doubt someone is going to stumble on those bodies soon, if not already and Valentine's men likely check in with a central point every thirty minutes or so, when that check doesn't come, questions are going to be asked and I'll have a whole new problem to deal with.

Death didn't scare me, little did, but it would complicate the matter.

"Wren, lower the gun and we'll do the same," I try to reason.

"How about you get the fuck out of my apartment before I shoot you."

"You're not going to shoot me," I growl, "if you were, you would have done it already."

Suddenly she pulls the trigger and a vase behind me smashes into thousands of pieces.

"And here I thought your aim was good," I taunt.

"I was aiming for the vase," she spits, "That was your last warning."

I have no doubt that shot would have woken half the building.

"You're pissing me off, little girl. Put the gun down."

She laughs, "You think you scare me?"

"I should," I rush her, darting left to right to avoid any bullets she does try to shoot my way. A loud pop sounds and pain slices through my arm.

Bitch shot me. She fucking shot me.

My shoulder rams into her stomach and we tumble, her back slamming into the wall behind her hard enough that the frames fall from the hooks and smash on the floor. She must have dropped the gun with the impact so now she's using any tool she can get her hands on. A hard object collides with the side of my head and I feel the skin split near my hairline, followed by a warm trickle of blood.

My patience shatters. In a move too quick for her to counter my hands go around her throat, squeezing.

I press up, straddling her hips, my fingers squeezing around her windpipe, the heels of my hands pressing down hard enough it could crush her neck. Fear flashes in her eyes as her fingers claw at my skin, her nails drawing blood as they drag through the thin flesh on the top of my hands.

Fuck this girl likes to make me bleed. I feel a steady stream of hot liquid rolling down my arm and face though the pain has been dulled by the adrenaline, pumping my system like a drug.

Ryker stands behind me, silent, simmering…

I press harder on her throat, her eyes become saucers, the blood vessels begin to pop as she tries and fails to draw oxygen into her lungs. I feel the strength starting to seep away from her body.

I'm going to kill her. I *was* killing her.

Her hands fall away from my wrists and to the sides, the limp limbs hitting the hard wood floors beneath us with a dull thud.

"Lex!" Ryker suddenly yells, breaking the trance of taking another life and he bolts forward though he is too late. I make out the shape of a long silver blade, but I quickly recognize the object to simply be a letter opener though it's as sharp as a knife as it slices through my thigh, cutting through the skin like butter and penetrating deep into the muscle.

"Fuck!" I bellow, my hands releasing her throat to stem

the bleed.

She chokes but the fight has left her, leaving her weak beneath me. With a quick jerk, the butt of the gun slams into her temple and finally – *fucking finally* – she closes her eyes.

4

Wren

Pain thumps through my skull and my throat feels as if I've swallowed a thousand razor blades. Groggily, I force my eyes to open, my lashes are stuck together, only when I lift my hand to rub them I can't. I pull my arm again, the sound of metal on metal scraping against my eardrums. What the fuck?

My ankles are in much the same state. Shackled.

Okay, don't panic. This could be a dream, a sleep paralysis perhaps but I know I need to figure it out. The feel of the metal against my skin seems too real to be just a dream and even as I will it not to come, the dread of what this means settles into the pit of my stomach. I know already that this is not a dream.

It all comes back in a reel of images.

Alexander Silver.

His gun pointed at my head, my own at his.

The fight.

His hands around my throat, the press of his weight against my own as he attempted to steal away the breath in my lungs.

Shit. What the fuck have I gotten myself into and how do I get out of it?

I try to peer around the room but there's no light and no windows at all. It's cold, the air tinged with damp and dust but there's something else, something old and rotten that makes me choke. Pushing down the need to gag I breathe through my mouth and settle my head back. The pain is a constant pulse, both inside my head and in various points in my body. The fucker hit me.

I don't know how long I lay there in the dark but eventually a door opens, allowing light to spill into the room. Instinctively, I narrow my eyes to stop the sting and allow them to adjust. A huge figure fills the door frame, so large it almost blocks out the light, the shoulder width alone almost touching each side of the frame.

"She's awake," his voice is rough, husky in a way that suggests he's a smoker or a man who doesn't use his voice all that often.

He steps to the side to allow another man in, with the light at his back I can't see his features, shrouded in shadow but he's big too, probably the same size as the first man but this one has an air of violence that surrounds him. An aura of menace that rings as a warning to anyone who bears witness to his presence.

There's something in the set of his shoulders, the way his hands dangle loosely at his sides, so very relaxed in a sea of chaos and violence.

I immediately know who I'm staring at, even if I can't see his face.

When he came up to me in the club my hackles instantly went up. My instincts were very rarely wrong, and they certainly didn't fail me on this occasion.

This man was dangerous.

No, he was more than dangerous, he's the monster under your bed, the villain in your stories. He's the motherfucking devil in the flesh.

I grit my teeth, was he here to finish the job? I uselessly pull at the shackles restraining me, feeling the metal biting into my skin, grazing and cutting away at my flesh.

I had no idea what they even wanted with me, the only connection I can think of is my father. I knew he was dodgy, but this... fuck, what even is this?

"Hello, Wren," his bourbon smooth baritone rolls over me, both a caress and a slap.

"Let me go, you asshole!"

He chuckles, "I like the fire in you."

"Come here," I hiss, "let me show you just how much fire I have."

"We've already danced this dance, little bird," he steps closer, an edge of steel to his tone, "it didn't work out so well for you."

I avert my eyes, allowing a smirk to tilt up my lips, pushing as much condescending snide into my voice as I say, "how's the arm? Or was it the leg?" My eyes flick back to where he stands above me, allowing them to roll over his tall, muscular frame.

He growls, a noise neither belonging to man or beast.

A tinkle of laughter leaves my throat but a wince cuts it off short as the pain there radiates through my neck, stifling me.

"Once we're done here," he steps forward and I notice the limp, how he holds himself and favors his left leg. Good, I hope it fucking hurts, "there won't be even an ember of life left in you. You can keep your fire now, Wren, but just know, I'll snuff those flames out quicker than you can even blink."

I had no doubt about it. I won't be leaving here alive. It was a given considering *who* I was dealing with.

That should terrify me. It should shake me down to my core, but all I feel is a fury building inside of me that makes me want to rip out of these cuffs and watch the life drain from his eyes.

He steps to the side of the bed I'm restrained to and reaches forward, brushing hair away from my face in a move too soft for a man who holds this much malevolence. "Touch me again," I breathe through the anger, "and I'll bite your finger off."

"Aren't you quite the savage, little bird," he comments, "Such a shame you're on the wrong side."

What?

I don't have time to answer when he turns and stalks out the room, shutting the door behind him, plunging me into a darkness so deep I wouldn't even be able to see my hand in front of my face.

The next visitor to come to my room is neither Lex nor the other man, instead it's a woman. She's lithe, tall with long blonde hair that's been pulled back from her face tightly. She's dressed in tight black pants and a tight top that follows the shape of her body like a second skin. I spot the gun tucked into the back of her trousers.

Ocean blue eyes meet mine and she quirks a brow, "Not that you could, but I wouldn't even think about it."

Her voice is melodic, but I quickly realize it doesn't match the owner. Her face remains impassive as she pushes my head roughly to the side and when she presses her red manicured fingers to my temple with no sense of empathy, a burst of pain has me hissing through my teeth.

"Did a number on you, huh?" She reaches into a box I hadn't noticed she'd bought in with her and presses something to my head, more pain, the pulse of it throbbing through my skull.

"Get the fuck off me," I growl.

"Quite the mouth you have there," she comments, amusement lacing her tone and tipping up her lips.

My nostrils flare.

I needed to get the fuck out of here. I had no idea what these guys wanted or who they were, but I knew a predator when I saw one. If I don't get out now, I doubt I'll be breathing for much longer. My death wouldn't be quick, it would be a torturous event dragged out over days. When the girl is done, she stands and exits the room but comes back a moment later holding a tray of food and a bottle of water with a straw in the top.

I quirk a brow, "What are you, their little pet?"

"Ha," she laughs, "by the way, you want to *not* give me all the attitude, I'm the reason you're even getting to eat."

"I'm not hungry."

"Fine," she thrusts the bottle at me, the straw hitting my bottom lip, "Drink."

I turn my head away.

She tuts loudly and stands from the bed, "Very well."

But those weren't parting words, instead she proceeds to stand and pour the entire bottle of water over my face.

I inhale automatically and then choke as the water hits my throat.

With no more words, she leaves the room and shuts the damn door again, plunging me into that void of darkness.

44

The silence and the dark will surely drive me crazy way before they get around to doing whatever it is they want to do.

I needed to get out.

The sudden burst of determination has me thrashing on the bed, tugging at my restraints. I'm pretty sure they're handcuffs, though I can't be sure without seeing them, and every time that door opens, I'm too distracted to get a good look.

Come on. Focus Wren.

I think back to all the training I've done with Griffin. All the hours I've been forced to endure in self-defense, trying to remember if I was taught how to get out of different types of restraints.

I remember being taught how to pick the locks or even shimming but that won't work here, I can't get to them, even with my fingers. I tug my hands down hard, the metal of the cuff biting into my skin. Pain slices through my wrists as the metal carves at my flesh, bruising, pinching, but unless I can break my own hand, I'm not getting out.

I thrash my head down, wincing with the pain that fires through the back of my skull and blow out a frustrated breath. I suppose I should be thankful for the training. I wonder if my father knew something like this would happen, and that's why he forced it for all these years so I could protect myself in this kind of event. Not a lot of good it does now, mind you.

If that were the case, it really begs the question as to what it is he does in his spare time. Me and my dad didn't exactly have a loving relationship and my mother was long gone. The training taught me to remain calm, fight but also raise hell if I must. And I wanted to raise hell. Who said dying had to be peaceful?

I scream. My throat pulls tight, turning from a wail to a croak too quick for my liking, but I don't stop.

"Hey!" I yell. "Oi, you fuckers!"

I thrash my arms and legs, clanging the metal of my restraints against the metal posts so the noise echoes through the empty room.

"Hey!"

I scream and yell for what feels like hours and finally the door slams open, "What!?" It's the same rough husky voice from before.

"I have to pee."

"Are you serious right now?"

"Oh I'm sorry," I snap, "I didn't realize that the normal bodily function would just stop because you guys said so."

The guy stomps across the room, "Why are you wet?"

"Oh, I have the bitch you sent in before to thank for that."

He growls something I don't quite catch but fishes into his pockets for keys. Okay, good. He's going to let me out and if I can get out, I can run.

He slides the key into the left lock and frees my hand

but before I can do anything, he twists my body and promptly cuffs it to the arm still restrained on the other side.

"This is a little much don't ya think?" I push sweetness into my voice, "Little old me can't do much harm."

"Ha," he shakes his head as he removes the other cuff, forcing my arms down. I peer down to see the gleaming silver around both wrists, secured together.

"Nice cuffs," I say, "is there something you're not telling me? Are you guys secretly some weird bondage society?"

He doesn't answer as he removes the cuffs from my legs and forces me to stand by yanking on my elbow. I get up, swaying a little as the blood rushes around my body from where I've been in the prone position for too long.

I stumble forward but he catches me quickly, keeping me upright as I'm dragged from the small dark room. We step out into a narrow hall with only a set of steps that lead upwards. He makes me go first, pressing into the small of my back.

"No funny business," he tells me.

I roll my eyes, "Jesus Christ."

The door at the top suddenly opens and the chick from before comes into view. She smirks and lets me pass before falling into step beside the guy who let me out.

They're silent and eventually I come to a junction at the end of the hall. I realize I'm in a house, a big one, one that screams money and power. Expensive art hangs from the walls, Persian rugs line the mahogany floors and crystal chandeliers dangle from the high ceilings, prisms of colour dancing across the white walls as a breeze teases the little diamonds. I've been around wealth my entire life but this is a whole other level.

"Left," Gruff orders.

I turn left, my bare feet squeaking on the polished floor.

"That door there."

I stop in front of it, waiting for them to open it. When neither of them does I turn my attention to them, "What do you expect me to do? Open it with my teeth?"

"I like her," the girl suddenly declares, stepping forward and opening it for me. I step inside, using my heel to kick it shut but it's stopped before it can click closed.

"Oh I don't think so," the girl says, stepping in with me.

"I can't pee with you in here."

She rolls her eyes, "Do your business, this isn't a luxury we give to most *guests*."

"Oh, I suppose being cuffed to the bed is also five star treatment."

"Would you prefer we dangle you from the ceiling? It can be arranged."

"You're all fucking crazy."

"No, we're fucking Silvers and it's about time you learned your place."

5

Lex

"Valentine," I drawl, kicking my legs up onto the desk, swirling the whiskey in my glass so the ice clinks against the edges.

"Give her back."

No greeting, how very rude.

"I see you got my message."

"Oh, I got your message, you sick son of a bitch, Wren has nothing to do with this."

And this is where he's going to fail. There's his weakness, like a beacon for my eyes. Little Wren Valentine is his absolute weakness, one that'll destroy him. Just as I planned. It's like exposing a jugular to a predator and in this game of predators it is always going to be me who comes out on top.

"Oh, I think she has everything to do with this, though I'm confused."

49

Heavy breathing on the other end of line puffs in my ear but he doesn't say anything else, so I continue.

"I will give it to you, you kept her a secret for a long time, I'm impressed actually, not a lot escapes me." I tip the whiskey to my lips before bringing it back down to dangle between my fingers.

"Give her back." I don't miss the way his voice lilts at the end, a barely restrained anger though I don't hear concern, just rage and that piques my interest. He doesn't seem concerned with her well being, he hasn't asked how she is or if she is even still alive, only that he wants her back. I keep this all to myself, I'll get to the bottom of it, one way or another.

"It wasn't until a little piggy squealed that I figured it out. At first, I thought she was staying with you, that she knew exactly who you were, but I've come to realize she's completely and utterly innocent."

Innocent wouldn't have been the word I would have used to describe her, not when the little she devil shot me and continues to fight me at every turn, but he doesn't need to know that. She may come across as the perfect little doll, smart, composed but I see beneath all of that. I see the fight, the fire, the lust for vengeance. It's one hell of an aphrodisiac, watching a strong woman fight and not bow down, witnessing the unadulterated fury in her stare as she watches you, calculating all the ways she may hurt you should she break free from her restraints. Just the thought of her fighting me has my cock hardening. In this life, you don't get anywhere by rolling onto your back, had she been on the right side of the line she would have made one hell of a companion.

"How does that feel, Valentine?" I didn't usually toy with my victims, but Marcus Valentine was a different breed. This fucker is going to pay for everything he's done to the Silver family and its interests. I'll make the asshole pay with more than just his blood.

He probably didn't realize it when he walked into this city all those years ago just who he was playing with, but he's soon going to find out he's swimming with sharks.

"What do you want?" Negotiation is his first point of call.

"Nothing."

"Money? The trade? My suppliers?"

I roll my eyes even though he can't see me, "I know each and every one of your transactions, Valentine, but don't you worry, I have that handled along with your little princess."

"Silver!" He growls. "You're fucking with something bigger than you."

I wonder how far he'll go to free the little bird. Not that I have any intention of letting the girl go but playing with him is appealing.

"Goodbye now, Valentine. You have yourself a nice night."

Is this really how we deal with shit in this family? No. It is not, my father would be furious but I'm in charge now and it's my city to rule as I see fit.

Innocent blood is going to be spilt, it's inevitable and I've quickly learned how to push pass that guilt, it doesn't affect me.

I do what I need to do for the success of this family, for these men and women working for me.

I hang up the phone and drain the rest of my glass, savoring the sweet burn as it rolls down my throat. My first taste of revenge against the Valentine's leaves me salivating for more. Standing from the chair in my office, I stretch out my muscles and cross the room, swinging the door open only to find echoes of a fight meeting my ears. Grunts and thuds travel down the long narrow halls of the house, meeting me where I stand in the threshold of my office.

For fucks sake, what now?

I follow the sound and stop short when I see Ainsley on her back, eyes closed, unconscious and Ryker and Wren going at it in the hallway outside the bathroom.

I leave them for five fucking minutes.

Ryker should know better.

"Enough!" I boom.

Ryker's back goes ramrod straight and even Wren has stopped, turning her attention to me. Her eyes narrow and her lips curl back enough to show me her teeth, and just to spite me no doubt, she raises her knee, hard, and hits my second in command in the dick. When he's hunched over, she jumps onto his back and pulls the chain securing her cuffs to his throat.

Seriously.

This chick is batshit crazy.

Ryker huffs impatiently but she tugs back, cutting off his air supply. He looks to me for approval and a slight nod of my chin gives him everything he needs to finish this off.

With his bulky frame, he throws himself back and slams her into the wall. It startles her enough for the grip on his throat to loosen, and as she tries to readjust Ryker uses the distraction to bend at the waist with enough momentum to throw her over his shoulders and head and onto the hard wood flooring.

She lands flat on her back in the middle of the hall, hair splayed around her head.

Winded, she stays there, sucking in a breath as I start towards her, leg twinging with pain from where she stabbed me.

I peer down at her, "I believe we're due a chat, little bird."

"You don't say," she wheezes. "You know people are going to miss me, the cops are probably already on it."

"I know they are," I nod, "but I've dealt with that, no one's coming to look for you."

Her eyes widen but she doesn't fight, it's almost like she's just realized she's got no hope here.

I reach down and haul her up. She's weak right now, dazed and injured which makes this a whole lot easier. I pick her up, cradling her to my chest. It would almost be intimate if we were anywhere else and I was *anyone* else. I ignore the pain in my arm and leg as I carry her, letting it fuel this need.

"I'm tired," she complains.

"It's not nap time, little bird."

"Stop calling me that," her words are slurred and I dare a glance down, her face is pale, lids hooded. She's slipping into unconsciousness. The hit to the end when she went down must have been harder than I thought.

Her head rolls back as her eyes slip closed.

I know Ryker will be tending to Ainsley so realizing I have no eyes on me, I detour and take her to a guest room on the top floor.

Why? I have no fucking idea.

When I lay her down on the bed I just stand and stare. Taking in her delicate features, the bow of her top lip, the plush bottom one and how her lashes cast long shadows over the apples of her cheeks. Her copper hair has since fallen out of the hold she had it in and it falls around her head like a halo. Long toned legs, skin milky and smooth. My eyes follow the lines of the tattoo on her thigh and then the one on her arm, intricately etched into her skin, delicate and feminine, a complete contrast to their owner.

There's something about her that interests me. Piques my curiosity and flames a well of heat inside my body that's completely inappropriate given the circumstances.

I hook my fingers beneath her chin and tilt her head, inspecting the bruise that has bloomed on her temple and the gash from where I hit her with the gun and then following the deep purple bruises around her throat.

Fuck.

I almost killed her.

Almost.

That wouldn't have been good, not when I needed her to see this through.

Still out cold, I shackle her to the bed so she can't get any ideas for when she does wake up and then I leave her there, heading back down.

Ryker is tending to Ainsley who is now awake and sat on the couch, leaning forward with her elbows resting on her knees.

"You underestimated her," I accuse.

"She's so small!" Ainsley grumbles and Ry laughs.

"I thought the same," he nods, frowning when his phone buzzes in his pocket. Pulling it out he checks the screen and then heads out the room, answering it.

I cock my head at Ainsley, the side of her face is red, turning purple as the bruising starts to take shape, "Not like you to pull down your guard, what happened?"

She shakes her head, "Won't happen again."

"Make sure of it."

She grumbles something and then stands, exiting the same way Ryker did and then I'm alone again.

Why the hell did I set her up in the bedroom?

This isn't a fucking hotel and she definitely is not a guest. She's the means to an end. Not even a bargaining chip.

She's revenge.

Cold hard revenge.

My words taunt me.

She's completely and utterly innocent.

They're not wrong.

It wasn't hard to figure out that he had sent her away when she was young, young enough for her not to remember who he was and put her with another guy in his inner circle so he could keep an eye on her and pull whatever strings necessary to ensure her life turned out the way he wanted it to.

I wasn't interested in the little guys. It was Marcus Valentine I wanted.

The only reason I even found out he had a daughter was because his men are weak as fuck and turned the moment I pressed a barrel to his temple. No loyalty. No integrity. That canary sang until he was blue in the face.

And I found Marcus' weakness.

Though I should have dug deeper. Pushed harder. I would have figured out quick enough she wasn't close with him. It struck me odd that she was staying at the Lawson house, he wasn't high up in Valentine's command which meant I wouldn't have looked at him twice unless I needed to. The intel I picked up didn't show the link to Lawson, only Valentine. I didn't dig deep enough.

That was a mistake I would never make again.

My impatience to finish this far outweighed all else.

I needed to move her back down to the room below, she's the enemy and I needed to treat her as such.

I head towards the door.

"Lex!" Ryker storms into the room, "We have a problem."

"What?" I bark.

"The warehouse is on fire, Valentine torched it."

"Fuck!"

Wren will have to wait, I grab my keys and the jacket discarded over the back of the chair and head out, Ryker falling into step behind me as I dial the fire chief.

"You better get that blaze under control," I growl down the line.

"Silver," Chief Donald Arthur was an old git and a grumpy bastard, and he made sure every damn time I called I knew he was unhappy to hear from me. I didn't care, he was a pawn as much as every other fucker in this city, sitting pretty in my pocket and to be called upon whenever I needed it, there wasn't a choice in the matter, "Who'd you piss off now?"

"I don't think you heard me, Arthur," I throw myself behind the wheel, Ryker climbing into the Range Rover next to me.

"My best guys are down there but it doesn't look good."

"Then you best make it look fucking good Arthur, I'm not fucking around here. You want to keep that job I suggest you fix this."

I have a million dollars' worth of drugs in that fucking warehouse damn it, and a shit ton of business will literally go up in smoke if it is not contained. With the next shipment not due in till next week, I can't afford the mess this will make.

Twenty minutes later I park the car in the lot outside the warehouse. The whole building is on fire, the sky around it lit up in an orange hue as the flames lick at the night sky. The blaze roars wildly and furiously, and there's no damn hope that the stock inside is still there.

The firefighters tackle the fire but it's no use.

Ryker steps up next to me, "A couple of guys saw Valentine's men come in with explosives and gasoline. They killed the guards and then torched the place."

"He wants his daughter back," I grumble.

"There's something else," he says.

I huff, "Of course there is."

He unlocks his phone and shows me a picture. It's one of my guys, head blown open but it's not that that has my attention. In the centre of his chest, held there with a blade buried into his flesh is a note.

Three days, Silver.

Give Wren back or I'll burn your entire world to the

ground.

A cruel smile curls at my lips, if he wants Wren back, he'll have to come get her himself. By the time he grows the balls to do so, she'll be dead.

6

Wren

Perhaps it was all a dream, a fucked up dream but a dream because this bed isn't the same one I've been in for the past God knows how long and this room is lit up with the moonlight streaming in through the window, casting shadows over the white painted walls and lighting up the paintings hanging there. I shift, feeling the silky sheets beneath my back and legs and almost groan at the luxury, even if my arms and legs have been restrained again and are slightly numb from being in this position for too long.

I wonder how many times I can take a hit to the head before I should start to worry about the lasting damage it's going to have.

Taking out the girl was easy, she had severely underestimated me and all it took was a swift elbow to stun her and then a knee to her temple and she went down. Gruff however was another matter. That fucker was big.

I gave it a good shot though, but there isn't going to be a next time for a while, I know that for sure. That was my only attempt at escaping, they won't make the same mistake twice.

My throat is as dry as a desert and my stomach rumbles, cramping with hunger.

How long have I been here now?

It's got to be days, three maybe but I have no idea, everything has blurred into one, making it impossible to tell one day apart from the next.

I lean back on the soft pillow under my head and take a deep breath.

The house around me is quiet, too quiet which is unnerving, and I still have no idea what they want with me.

Somewhere downstairs the door opens, and slams closed immediately before feet pound on the stairs, and then across the hall, loud and angry, heading right for me.

Great.

The door to the room smashes open, hard enough to vibrate the paintings hanging on the walls, and there he is.

There is something disturbingly beautiful about the man, he was lethal, unhinged and clearly batshit, but he was as brutal as he was beautiful. All sharp angles and hard lines. The scent of smoke and ash fills the room, getting stronger the closer he comes to the bed.

61

"Didn't peg you to be a smoker," I comment. That's the truth, his teeth are too white, too clean but then he clearly has money so the effects of smoking can just be wiped away.

"We're going to send a message, little bird," He growls down to me. Oh he's pissed.

"Okay, cool, why don't you hand me my phone and I'll get right on that."

Pushing him now seems like the wrong thing to do but I just can't help it. I've never been one to just take shit lying down, if there's a fight, I'm going to fight.

He withdraws a blade, turning it over in his hand, the steel catching in the light as he rolls it, pressing the sharpened edge against his palm hard enough to slice the skin and allow beads of crimson to bloom on the surface.

He smirks down at me, a cruel tilt of his lips that strikes fear right down to the pit of my soul. "You're funny."

"Thanks," I force the word from my lips as he leans forward and runs the very tip of that blade down the centre of my chest, the razor edge snagging and tearing the material of my clothes and further down to slice at my skin. The pain is almost a phantom, a sting barely present but it's there, nonetheless, making you uncomfortable, making you want to kick it away if only to ease the frustration of having it irritate you.

He follows the blade with his eyes as he moves it down my abdomen and then back up, all the way up until the tip sits right atop my pulse point, with every thump my wild heart gives, the blade pushes in further, drawing blood that wells and then rolls down my throat.

He appears to be hypnotized by the trail of blood, his silver eyes following it down as it rolls over my skin before his eyes bounce up and land on my mouth.

My lips are parted, my breathing shallow and fast, the warming between my thighs worrying and yet welcoming.

He brings the blade away from my neck, the silver now laced with red ribbons, a mixture of my blood and his and reaches forward, placing the very tip of it against my bottom lip. I'm frozen, unable to move as he watches me intently, not blinking, not moving except for the hand that holds the blade. Slowly, he pushes the blade down, the tip biting into my bottom lip and I have no choice but to open my mouth. There's a sting on the sensitive flesh where he's cut me, and I feel more blood rolling slowly over my lip and onto my chin.

His shoulders square and his spine straightens as the pupils of his eyes seem to devour his irises.

I'm prepared for him to cut me, to stab me, ready for whatever wound he's about to inflict. I see it there, a warning inside his eyes, a promise of violence and I only feel it sinking deeper into my body as he draws closer, taking the blade away from my mouth quickly, the edge slicing through my lip before he places it back at my throat, pressing it against the windpipe. There should be pain, but the threat of death simply numbs everything and knowing that a simple jerk of his hand will end it for me keeps the panic and fear behind a barrier. His eyes bounce between my eyes, my mouth and the blade pressing into my flesh. All the air leaves my lungs, a tightening in my stomach that really didn't belong in this situation. Instinctively, I swallow, the move making the blade scratch against my skin and just when I think this is it, he's going to snatch that blade through my neck his mouth slams against mine with a ferocity that I am not prepared for.

I should fight.

I need to fight, bite him, headbutt him but I don't do that. Of course I don't because my body has turned against me, and I tilt my head to let his tongue stroke deeper.

One hand still holds that damn blade to my throat but the other grips my hair and tugs, pulling painfully but instead of lashing out like I should, I whimper and purr like a damn cat.

My arms pull at the restraints, my legs curl and heels dig into the mattress, my back arching towards him. The threat of injury from the knife and the way his tongue lashes at mine creates a mixture deadlier than any weapon he could use against me.

He yanks away from me, abruptly, withdrawing both himself and the blade and simply stares down at where I'm a mess on the bed, restrained and confused. The metallic taste of blood sits on my tongue. His jaw pulses as he clenches his teeth and without a single word, he sheaths the knife, keeping his eyes holding mine, and withdraws his phone, snapping a picture before spinning on the heel of his shoe and exiting the room.

My lips tingle from the kiss, my body coiled up tight as heat continues to pulse low in my belly. I try to press my thighs together but the damn ankle cuffs stop me from being able to squash the sensations.

This is not normal. Clearly the knocks I've had to my head in the last few days have already taken hold.

Lex

I stare down at the image, the blood smeared across her throat, her chin and mouth, eyes wide and confused, staring right at me whilst I stand above her. I hit the send button.

He wants to play fucking games, we'll play games.

But what the fuck did I do?

Kissing her.

Shit.

I still taste her on my tongue, taste her blood, feel the soft pillowy mouth yielding beneath mine with my blade pressed to her throat. The soft little mews and whimpers fueled me to go harder, hoping, like the sick son of a bitch that I am, that she would fight a little, let the blood roll and the violence add fuel to whatever fucked fire is burning between us.

I shake my head to dislodge the thoughts and fall down onto the couch, resting my glass in the centre of my chest.

I inhale the smoky scent surrounding me, a mixture of the fire and the whiskey in my glass.

I went into that room prepared to break her. I was ready to crush her, crush her pretty little wings and any fire she may still have burning. Use it to send a better message but I kissed her instead. Fuck.

I throw the remaining liquid in the glass down my throat and then proceed to launch the glass at the wall. It smashes, raining shards of crystal all over the fur rug that sits in front of the fireplace.

I didn't live here. Fuck that. This was the compound, a safe house, set far away from the city with no prying eyes or nosy neighbors. It was guarded to high heaven with cameras all over the ground, a security system at the gate and sensors to alert me of any unwanted visitors trying to break through the perimeters. It seemed the best option to bring Wren to, but I want my penthouse.

I want to look down at the city below through the floor to ceiling windows that stretch the entire way around the suite, I want to feel the power in my veins, see my empire at my feet.

I feel weak right now. Fucking weak and that's not a feeling I want to have for long.

I had hoped to drag this out a little, really make Marcus beg before I put both him and *her* out of their misery but I'm not sure I can last much longer.

I knew Valentine would try to make good on his threat which is why I've doubled the man power across the city at every location the Silver family own plus on the streets.

Marcus Valentine had been a cockroach from the very start, a dirty little snake that thought he would take the

South side of the City. He was small at first and my father chose to negotiate rather than take out the problem. For a few years that was fine, they put their business through us, we controlled their connections, the supplies, dealings and negotiation but at some point Marcus slipped through the net.

He found allies in our enemies, grew his circle, his connections. I still have no idea which of the fuckers it is that supported him and funded his desire to take over the city but once he was dealt with, I'd find them, and I'd end them.

When my father found out Marcus was going behind our back he paid him a visit.

The thing about my father was, he truly was ruthless, brutal even but he wanted some semblance of peace in the city, so he tried to renegotiate.

Men died.

War started.

It was a year after that, six months ago that Marcus hit my fathers house whilst they were throwing a party.

We didn't involve the citizens, especially not the ones that kept the businesses running and the cops looking the other way but that's what he did.

The Police chief died that night and the resulting pain of having to renegotiate with the new guy that filled his place was long and frustrating.

Everyone has secrets, you just had to find the ones worth using.

Threats and violence only worked sometimes. It didn't matter if they hated me or what I stood for, it didn't matter if they loathed the fact that I held the true power in this city, despite their titles and appearance of authority, long as they stayed in line.

Everyone has a place and me, along with the Silver name and the ones closest stand on fucking top.

7

Wren

What I wouldn't give right now for a nice stroll in the park. My legs ache from being still for so long and with my arms pinned above my head the blood can't circulate properly meaning my fingers tingle every time I move them.

I'm starving too. My stomach cramps painfully and I blow out a frustrated breath. The sun is blaring through the window, the sky a perfect cloudless blue. Every now and then a bird will fly passed the window but other than that, it's completely silent and still. I tilt my head and sniff.

Jesus. A shower would be nice.

The need to get out of here was still as strong as ever but I had no idea how I was going to manage it. I've been alone more than I've had company and still no idea why I'm here.

It all leads back to my dad, of course it does but whatever it is he did, it doesn't look like their willing to negotiate with me or even share the information.

I wonder if he's fighting for me at all. I wonder if he knows it's Alexander Silver who has me.

When the door opens to the room I don't bother looking up. I just lay there staring at the ceiling, waiting for whoever it is to step into view.

Alexander stands at the side of the bed, looking down at me. He's dressed in a pristine charcoal grey suit, his unruly hair falling over his forehead. His hands are buried into the pockets of his trousers, causing the jacket he has on to open a little, showing the handle of his Glock. There's no tie to finish the look, just the two top buttons of his white shirt open, showing off bronzed skin. My tongue traces the cut in my bottom lip, the sting of it making me wince as I remember the way his mouth felt when it was on mine, hard, unforgiving and all consuming. Even if I don't want to remember how it made me feel, the thought of it still warms me through, how dangerous it was, how fucking dirty...

"It appears we've hit a bit of an impasse, Little bird," he says quietly, crouching until his eyes are level with mine. Lazily I roll my head to the side, sucking in a breath to prepare myself for his ruthless beauty.

It really isn't fair that a man like him has been graced with such looks. He's a wolf, beautiful and yet deadly, one snap of his teeth and you'll lose a hand, or he'll simply rip your throat out. He isn't a man to be underestimated. There's this calm storm that seems to always blow around him, it doesn't appear to be harmful but then if you step into it, it'll sweep you away.

The man is the devil, in all his glory.

I knew it in the club, I knew it when I was staring down the end of his barrel, my own pointed at him, and I certainly knew it when his hands wrapped around my throat. He was fully prepared to kill me there and then, with his bare hands on my living room floor. Had I not stabbed him when I did, I had no doubt I'd be buried in an unmarked grave somewhere out in the sticks for the scavengers to dig up.

I swallow, but I refuse to fear him. I won't give him that power over me. I may be on the bottom here, but I'll never show it to him. He can keep me here all he likes, he can tie me up, he can even hurt me if he wants but I'll never give him my vulnerability.

Showing a weakness in front of this man would be like showing your jugular to a lion.

Foolish.

"Oh yeah?" My voice is croaky and hoarse from lack of use and hydration, and I swallow painfully, eyes watering with the pain, "how so?"

"It appears daddy wants to send a message," he rubs a hand across his scruff, his eyes rolling slowly over my body. I squirm under the heat of it.

I have to be all kinds of fucked up to get turned on by him.

But the clenching in my belly and the ache between my thighs tells me all I need to know.

He may be a monster but I'm the depraved little girl too curious to heed the warnings ringing in my head, wanting to know exactly how it would feel to be fucked by a man like Alexander Silver.

"What message?"

So he was looking for me and negotiating perhaps?

"Well he set one of my warehouses on fire." Alexander rolls his head, cracking his neck.

I can't hide my shock at that news. I couldn't imagine the man I knew as my dad to set anything on fire. He looked too tidy to get dirty himself, I'm sure he had men to do that for him.

"Interesting."

Alexander quirks a brow, "I lost a lot of money you know."

"I'm sure you have more to spare a few thousand."

"Try a few million."

"What did he want to say?" I change the subject.

"I have three days," he smirks.

"To do what?"

"Return you."

"Or what?"

"He'll burn my whole world to the ground."

Silence settles between us. I don't have anything to say

to him. He continues to stare at me, eyes holding my own and I don't want to break it, I don't, but the look seers me to the soul, it has my brain scrambling and my body trying to keep up.

I drop my eyes. He laughs.

Asshole.

"I don't take threats all that lightly, little bird."

"Aw," I snap, "Did someone hurt your feelings?"

"There it is," he grins so suddenly it catches me off guard but is gone in a second.

"Fuck you, Alexander Silver."

"Maybe if you're lucky."

He unfolds his body, "Seeing as I only have you for three more days little bird, it's time to start planning."

"You're going to let me go?" I feel idiotic to allow so much hope into my voice but it's there, a lilt in my tone that wasn't there moments ago.

"Oh no, little bird. I'm sending my own message."

I watch him cross the room and stop in the door, his massive body filling the frame. He tilts his head, looking at me from over his shoulder, "Someone will be up shortly with food and then I'll allow a shower. Don't bite their fingers off."

"How chivalrous of you."

He leaves then, with the echo of his soft laughter

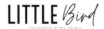

bouncing down the hall.

Sure enough, a woman enters the room carrying a bowl of soup and bread. The smell of tomato and basil hits my nose and I practically drool, salivating at the thought of food.

"Can you release my hands so I can sit?" I ask the woman.

She looks about forty but not hard like the others, she doesn't respond to me, instead she takes the spoon and dips it into the red liquid.

"How am I supposed to eat if I'm led down?"

Again no answer. She pushes the tip of the spoon against my lip and begins to pour it into my mouth.

With a huff I open and hot soup hits my tongue. I groan as the taste bursts against my tastebuds, sliding down my parched throat far too effortlessly.

It goes down easily and quickly and when the woman breaks off a bit of bread to feed me, I shake my head, turning slightly so she can't force it.

"I've had enough, thank you."

She nods once and grabs the bottle of water and straw, holding it to my mouth.

I take it gratefully this time, sucking down half the bottle before she pulls it away and quirks a brow.

I shrug, as best I can in the current position and then she pushes it back to my mouth, allowing me to finish it off. It's ice cold and refreshing, quenching the thirst

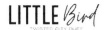
instantly.

After that's finished, she gets up and leaves. "Hey! Alexander told me I could shower!"

"You think we're going to let a housekeeper shower you?" It's Gruff's voice. I still haven't heard his name so he's still Gruff to me. It suits him, he's a beast of a man, one you'd likely find chopping wood somewhere far in the mountains. His beard is groomed, his hair long but slicked back. He's dressed similarly to Alexander, his suit black rather than grey and I have no doubt he's packing too.

"Well you're not showering me," Gruff flashes me a grin.

"Don't knock it till you try it."

"I'd like to maintain at least a little dignity, dickhead."

"Come on," he makes quick work of the cuffs, and instead of putting them in front of me when he restrains me again, he puts them behind my back, so tight it pulls my shoulders, my muscles protesting at the unnatural angle.

"I can still use my feet you know," I tell him smugly, "I could break your neck just as easily."

His warm chest presses into my back, "Lex might be stalling to put a bullet in your head, but I won't hesitate little girl."

I tuck that little bit of information down about the stalling and snicker, "But you won't."

"Why's that?"

I was baiting him but if I was going to die anyway, what did it matter?

"You're too scared to disobey your master."

He growls menacingly behind me.

"Am I wrong?"

I'm shoved hard, losing balance I hit the hard wood floor on my knees, pain vibrating up my thighs and hips.

"How someone hasn't cut your tongue out already is beyond me." Gruff grumbles, tugging me back to my feet. The quick glance I get of his face I swear I see a smile but that can't be right.

The bathroom we stop at is on the same floor as the room I'm being held in and it's huge, a clawfoot tub sits in the centre with brass taps, and off to the left, up against the far wall is a marble vanity, the mirror above it taking up the entire wall, the gold frame intricately weaving over the sides and edges with vines and flowers. There's a shower big enough to fit four on the other side and a toilet. It smells floral in here, clean and I take a deep breath. Despite the situation, a shower is going to be delightful.

"You can leave now." I tell Gruff.

"I don't think so."

"I'm not showering in here with you!"

"You can always go without."

"No!"

Gruff laughs, crosses his arms and leans against the counter, watching me, daring me.

Is he serious right now?

I want to hit him but with these damn cuffs I can't do shit.

Frustration makes my eyes sting. Damn it, I'm not going to cry.

"I can't wait until I can wipe that damn smile off your face."

"You can try," he growls.

"Now, now," Alexander steps into the bathroom, amusement tilting up his delectable mouth. "Carry on Ryker, I might just let her take a shot at you. Now what's the problem this time?"

8

Lex

Wren stares at me like she would love nothing more than to rip my throat out with her bare hands. I believe she'd do it too.

What kind of man does it make me if that shit turns me on?

"Are you going to be good, little bird?" I ask, waiting to hear the tell-tale sound of the door clicking behind me. Ryker wasn't really going to stand in here with her, no, no, no one else gets to see her like this.

I try to think back to all the prisoners I've held in my keep and allowed them the comfort I've given her, but I think of none. The people I bring here are here for one reason. To die.

They've fucked up somehow and are being punished or they're simply a means to an end, just like Wren here is. Only I shouldn't be allowing her to shower, I shouldn't be feeding her and making sure she has comfort beneath her back and yet here I am, allowing her just that.

She glares at me, the rims of her nostrils flaring as she takes steady breaths.

"I'm going to uncuff you now," I tell her, "You'll be wise to behave yourself."

I cross the space between us and go behind her back, slotting the key into the cuffs, waiting for the click of the locking mechanism to release and then I pull them away. Red welts mark her flawless skin and she rubs at her wrists, fingers pushing against the marks.

My chest twinges.

What the fuck?

"Strip."

"Are you serious? You're not going to allow me some dignity?"

I quirk a brow. "No."

"Turn around."

"No."

A puff of air huffs from her mouth. "Why don't you just kill me now, huh?" She hollers, "You're gonna do it anyway, just get it over with!"

"All in time, little bird."

She visibly swallows, the first show of fear she's given me since I took her all those days ago. I don't like it.

But I don't like this feeling anymore either. There's something wrong with me, there has to be. The sickness that rolls in my gut, the twinges in my chest, I must be coming down with something. Just what I need.

I step forward.

"Touch a single finger on my body, Silver and I'll break every single bone in your hand."

"Don't kid yourself little bird," my hand cups her chin, fingers pressing into the soft tissue on her cheeks, "If I were to press these hands to any part of your body it's because you've begged me for it. You've pleaded."

Despite the hand that holds her face she still manages to lift her chin defiantly, showing me that pretty face.

"By the time a single finger runs through your pussy, you'll be slick and wet and wanting for what I'd have to give you."

Her eyes widen and her throat works on a swallow. I don't miss the way her thighs tremble, begging to be pressed together, if only to ease the ache between her legs. I can practically smell her arousal and that shit ain't good.

My cock jerks, fully prepared to slide balls deep inside of her and have her screaming my name.

"You want that little bird?" I tease through gritted teeth, my fingers pressing harder.

"Stop calling me that," She breathes, no heat to her words. She secretly likes it and hates that she does.

It's no doubt confusing being attracted to me. The man that almost killed her only a few days ago, the same man that kidnapped her and strapped her to a bed in a strange house, giving little to no information as to why.

Completely and utterly innocent.

Those words taunt me.

I've made it my own personal mission to push all that shit away. There's no way to make it in the world with your humanity still in place. You take what you need, what you want, and you don't care who gets hurt in the process. You steal and you kill because that's what gives you the power. You drive fear into the people around you to maintain your authority.

But this. This *guilt*, it'll kill me well before I get a chance to harm her.

I'm standing so close I see the tones of red in her hair, the light dusting of freckles on her skin. I drag her towards me, dropping my head so my lips whisper against her skin.

Her chin is still tilted up defiantly inside my grip, her hands balled into fists at her sides.

"You can say it," I tell her on a whisper, running my tongue up the shell of her ear, "your secret is safe with me. You want me and you hate yourself for it."

She lashes out, swinging wide, on course for her fist to hit me square in the jaw. I catch it last minute, gripping her entire fist in my hand. I snatch my hand away from her face, pushing slightly so she stumbles away from me but don't release the fist inside my palm.

Ainsley was right, she's so small, this tiny fragile thing, easy to crush and yet she stands tall. She roars loudly, and holds herself as if she were the biggest person in the world. It's not hard to see why most people would underestimate her and she uses that to her advantage.

I squeeze her hand, not hard enough to break anything but it's going to hurt as her knuckles roll together and her fingers curl in too tightly. The edges of her eyes crease but other than that she gives no sign that she's in pain.

"You're such a brave girl," I tell her.

"And you're a pig."

I suck my bottom lip into my mouth, scraping my teeth across it before releasing it again. I let her go abruptly and take a step back before I do something stupid like kiss her again.

"Strip now, little bird, shower," I tell her, "I'm allowing you some semblance of normality before I take that away."

"That's cruel you know," she tells me, seeming to give up the fight for me to leave the room.

She tugs her shirt over her head, revealing tight and toned abdominal muscles. A silver bar glints in her naval, and there's another tattoo etched in her side over her ribs.

I realize my error immediately.

Her curves, all of them are on show to me right now, the dip in her waist, the flare of her hips. Her breasts are covered with a lace type of cropped top, resembling a bra but not quite as supportive. I don't know what they call it, but it hides nothing. I see the shapes of her breasts, her nipples showing through the translucent material. Her chest moves rapidly, her breath coming fast.

She moves to her little shorts next and tugs them down her toned legs, stepping out of them until she's left in just that tiny little bra and her panties.

Holy fuck.

I thought I'd felt pain before but staring at a woman like Wren and not being able to even touch her wasn't just damn painful. It was *torture.*

I tilt my chin towards the ceiling, staring down at the little bird in front of me, the fiery desire burning so hot and powerful in my veins it takes everything in me not to snap and rip the rest of those clothes from her body. I feel my nails biting into my palms, the sharp edges cutting through the skin to allow beads of blood to sink beneath the nailbeds.

Fuck.

I've witnessed nails being pulled from fingers, brains being splattered over the wall and yet I can't see a grown woman naked without reacting like an adolescent boy!?

It truly fucks me in the ass to watch her and want her and not touch her.

She keeps her green stare on my face, never once turning her back on the monster in the room and switches the shower on, allowing a few seconds for the water to heat before her bare feet squeak against the tile on the bathroom floor and she climbs under the spray, still in her underwear.

The glass steams up immediately and it's only then, when she has some protection from the fog on the glass that she removes the rest of her clothing, throwing the damp lace to the corner of the shower basin.

She stands under the spray, the water coming down powerfully and soaking her naked body. The glass has already steamed up, but I can see it all, the curve of her breasts, the way they push out as she arches her back and tips her face to the water.

Damn siren.

The water soaks her red hair, straightening out the curls and plastering them to her back. Her ass is curved and tight, perky, perfect for a hand to squeeze and caress and slap. She keeps her face tilted to the water, allowing it to wet her skin and roll over the surface, droplets rolling between her lips, clinging to her eyelashes.

Turning away, I cross to the vanity and grip the marble counter.

I can't just leave her in here on her own, fuck knows what kind of trouble she'd cause but if I stay in here any longer, I believe I might just join her in that shower. Have I ever been so tempted before?

No, there was never any need to be tempted, I could just have what I wanted.

But her, she's the damn enemy's daughter. The opposition. The fucker threatening my city.

Even the reminders aren't enough to push down the

compulsion.

She doesn't even know *who* she is. Why she is here.

I keep myself firmly planted at the counter, hands gripping the marble tight enough I'm sure I'm able to crack it but, even I know I'm not super human and this shit won't crack under the pressure unlike me right now.

Finally the shower turns off and the glass door opens.

I catch her reflection in the mirror above the vanity, and if I thought seeing her before was bad, seeing her like this is agony.

Wet skinned, droplets of water running over the curves, following all the lines of her body I wish my tongue could trace, red hair clinging to her back. Pink skinned, wide eyed.

So very innocent.

Shit.

Shit

9

Wren

There's something empowering about a man brought to his knees – figuratively of course – by your body. I see it as clear as day, he wants me, and it fucking kills him.

Good.

I hope seeing me tears him apart inside. I hope it turns his gut and forces his heart to pound uncomfortably.

What I'm not prepared for is my own desire burning hot as hell in the pit of my stomach. It's sick, it's twisted and yet no matter how hard I try to control it I want him just as badly.

If he's the monster, what kind of sick fuck does that make me?

The man kidnapped me for heaven's sake, I *stabbed* him and yet my pussy clenches, I grow wet, the lust making my head hazy and the lines between us become blurred.

One little taste wouldn't hurt, surely. Just a touch, a slight caress.

No.

I won't do it. He can continue to want me, he can continue to war with himself, but I won't give him the satisfaction, only for him to put a bullet between my eyes. Because that's how this is going to end. He hasn't said the words but I'm not stupid. There's no way I'm walking out of here with my heart still beating.

It's sad that my life will end at only twenty-three years old, but I don't fear the end.

I pluck a towel from the folded pile near the shower and secure it around my body before picking up another to knot around my hair, holding the wet tresses atop my head in a turban. Now covered, his eyes go back to that blank yet slightly amused stare.

"Are you finished?"

"Yes."

"Good."

Clipped, short and icy.

As I follow him back to my room a plan forms in my mind. The man wants me, that much is obvious and if I can get him close enough, maybe I can use it to my advantage. He carries a gun on him, probably other weapons too I just needed to find them.

I watch his formidable body, the way the muscles move

in his back and shoulders, how quickly his legs eat up the space before him. His wicked beauty is unfair, the brutal lines that make up his body means that this little war between us is unbalanced. A monster shouldn't look that good.

Back in the room, I look towards the bed, the sheets pristine and not the rumpled mess they were before. His housekeeper must have changed them since we had been gone.

"Can I trust you won't jump out the window if I leave the handcuffs off?"

"That depends," I shrug, heading towards the window to peer down. Three floors and a straight edge with absolute zero way of climbing down, no guttering or trellises in sight. If I jumped, I'd break both legs if not more.

When I turn back to Alexander he's grinning, a condescending and smug tilt of his lips. I roll my eyes.

"I won't be escaping out the window," I tell him.

"Good."

He says no more as he turns and heads towards the door, "There's some clean clothes in the drawers. Help yourself."

"You know this isn't how it's supposed to be," I call after him, "All this kindness is going to make me believe you have a heart after all."

"Don't be fooled, little bird, this isn't kindness, this is me simply," he purses his lips and rolls his head side to side as he chews over what words he wants to use, "offering you a little comfort before I have to take that away."

"So it will end that way then?" I say, keeping him in the room a little longer. When I don't elaborate, he places his hands in his pockets, arching a brow whilst he waits for me to continue.

I head to the drawers, pulling the top one open to find simple tank tops stashed within. I pluck a black one out and then move to the next drawer, grabbing a pair of sweats that are going to be too large for my frame. I'm short, only five foot three and a hundred and thirty pounds which makes buying clothes that fit me perfectly a hardship.

I get to the bed and then drop my towel.

"Fuck!" Alexander roars, eyes widening. I hold in my chuckle, slowly easing my legs into the sweats. As expected, they are too big so I tie them as much as I can and then roll both the waist band and the legs so I can move without tripping or the things falling to the floor. I slip the tank over my head, covering myself.

I continue to watch him, seeing how tightly his neck is strained as if barely withholding his restraint.

I sit at the edge of the bed, cocking my head as I watch him.

"I'd like to believe you're not the monster you come across as, but I also learned long ago what you see is usually what you get."

"You'd be wise to listen to your instincts, little bird, this kindness is from pity and nothing else. Do you think I'll feel guilty when I eventually have to do what I set out to do?"

"You know," I tap my finger to my lips, "in all of this, the threats, the conversations, not once have you stated the words 'I'm going to kill you.' Why is that?"

His eyes narrow, "You want me to lay it out?"

"Yes."

He crosses the room and stands in front of me, looking down at where I'm sat on the bed. I was already much smaller than him but in this position my eyes are level with his crotch.

A little thrill shoots through me.

My hormones clearly aren't getting the memo.

"You want me to say it?" He growls.

"Yes."

Suddenly his hand comes around my throat and he shoves me onto the bed, flat on my back with his weight pressing into me. My thighs cradle his hips and I don't miss the hardness pressing into my clit through the material of the sweats. Arousal floods me and my hips grind against the sensation, needy and wanton despite knowing how dangerous this is.

Damn it.

His pupils are blown, eyes that were once silver appear black with only a neon rim, haloing his pupils. His nostrils flare and his fingers twitch, but he isn't pressing hard on my windpipe, I can still breathe perfectly fine. The pain of the bruising there already makes my eyes water but it doesn't take away from the sensation going on down there, especially not when I feel his own hips roll to mimic the movements of my own.

"Why say it when I can show you exactly what I plan to do?" His voice is all animal, a growl, husky, rough, the vibrations of it travelling from his chest into mine.

I tip my chin back defiantly and his eyes drop to my lips.

"Then do it," I tell him on a whisper.

I press my hips up harder eliciting a moan, whether it's from him or me I don't know.

His lips crash down on mine, with his hand still placed around my throat, and right in this moment I'm his willing captive, the delusional little girl begging to be touched.

Escape. Live.

The words push in at the corners of my mind, through the fog of lust running wild inside of me, I realize how much of an idiot I am being. His tongue duels with mine, heavy with shameless need and desire and I match the pace, pushing back. I dust my fingers up his side, feeling the muscles jump under my fingertips beneath his shirt and I follow them around to his back. The hard butt of his gun hits the heel of my hand, but I don't linger long enough for him to realize I've felt it. I just need to get it. I pull the bottom of his shirt from his pants, digging in my nails. He nips my bottom lip and I almost lose it. His teeth sink into the plump, sensitive flesh and a very real moan leaves me.

Fuck, I've never been so damn hot for a guy. It just so happens that the guy I'm suddenly fucking batshit for is the same guy destined to end me.

Quickly, before I allow this to go any further, my hand curls around the gun and I yank it from its place, finding the safety catch easily. I press it into his side, pushing hard enough to leave a mark.

He kisses me one last time before he chuckles, lifting his face away from me.

His eyes bore down into me and a dark smudge of a brow lifts.

"Up," I order. "Now."

Slowly, he eases off of me, adjusting himself but I see the stiff rigid length of him pressing angrily against his zipper. I know exactly how hard he is for me right now.

Yeah buddy, I think to myself as I push up off the bed, *I'm just as hot for you too.* In all the crazy shit I've done in this life, this has to take the cake. Not the gun levelled in his direction, the indecision on whether this is the right thing to do.

Crazy bitch.

I push the thoughts aside, standing from the bed with the gun still pointed in his direction, I try to steady my breathing.

"House is awfully quiet," I comment.

"I sent them away," he nods.

"That was silly, whatever will you do now without your trusty sidekick?"

"Ryker is my second, not my sidekick," he corrects, "and if he finds me dead there isn't a place in this world you can hide where he won't find you."

"Oh I believe that," I nod, "but that's okay."

"You're brave," he nods, "a little stupid but brave."

I narrow my eyes, "How am I stupid, Alexander?"

He chuckles, "Damn, when you say my name like that it gets me real hot." As if to prove himself he palms his cock through the material of his pants.

I'm staring. I know I am, but I can't fucking stop.

"Answer the question," I grit out, "how am I stupid?"

"Are you going to shoot me, little bird?"

"Yes."

"And that there is where your foolishness is," he rubs a hand across his kiss swollen lips, "because if you had really thought about this, do you honestly believe that I would have kept a loaded gun within reach of your greedy little hands?"

My eyes widen, he's bluffing.

My finger twitches on the trigger and he just grins wider, the sick bastard. He's taunting me, has to be, to save his own skin.

"Go ahead," he nods, "shoot me."

Do it, Wren. Shoot him.

The muscles in my hands cramp up, why the hell can't I do this!? Damn it!

"Pull the trigger."

My heart thumps wildly in my chest, my stomach churns.

"Do it, Wren, pull the trigger! Shoot me!"

He steps forward and I press the trigger.

10

Lex

The click is loud, deafening really, second to the sound of her heavy breaths. Her eyes are wide, swollen lips parted.

My cock is harder than it has ever been before, pressing painfully on the zipper of my pants.

The girl pulled the trigger with the gun aimed at my head. She was prepared to do it so, why the fuck am I hotter than hell for her?

I take calm steps towards her when really, all I want to do is rush her and strip her from the clothes she's only just pulled on. I'm not thinking straight and right now I don't want to be. All I want is to be balls deep inside this fucking crazy woman.

She presses the trigger again and again, frantically, so much so that the gun isn't even pointed at me anymore.

I wasn't stupid to leave my own gun on me loaded.

There was always a chance this could happen, even if the kiss didn't occur, and I have so many weapons stashed around the house I wouldn't be unarmed for long. Right now I am weaponless. Did I need a weapon to take her out? No, of course not, doesn't mean I wouldn't come out of it bleeding though. I'm sure the girl will put up a hell of a fight

In fact, I hope she does. When it eventually happens, and it will, she better fucking fight. She deserves to give herself that much.

I step into the gun, the barrel pressed to my sternum as I reach forward and tilt her chin up so she can see my face. Her eyes are wide, swimming with panic but not fear. This was her plan. Seduce and take out.

The little siren.

"Brave girl," I murmur, leaning forward to whisper my lips across hers. She allows it, her lashes fluttering closed. Her copper hair, darker now it's wet, is pushed away from her angelic face, falling down her back with little droplets of water rolling over the strands and dripping off the ends to soak into the fresh sheets below. "But very misbehaved."

I pry the gun from her hands, but she doesn't let go so easily. When it finally comes away, she whimpers against my mouth.

"Do you want to feel good, little bird?" I mumble, dipping my head to her throat.

She doesn't answer me, but she doesn't pull away either.

"I need words," I tell her.

"Y-yes."

"Good girl."

I tuck my fingers under the hem of her tank and push it up, feeling her silky smooth skin under my hands. She's burning hot, her skin feverish and soft. I discard the tank behind me, leaving her top half bare to my eyes. She's so fucking perfect. Curves in all the right places, a taut belly and her breasts sit perky and round on her chest. My fingers feather on the underside, a swarm of goose bumps pimpling her skin. Her nipples are hard pebbles, begging for my touch. I follow the curve of her breasts, watching and reveling in the way she arches her spine and pushes them forward for me.

"So very pretty," I mumble.

Her breathing comes out faster as I roll a nipple between my thumb and forefinger, pinching hard enough to straddle the line between pleasure and pain.

She might not realize it yet, but this girl likes a fight with her pleasure. I just know it.

I'll push and she'll push just as hard back.

"Stay still," I order, dipping my head to capture a nipple between my teeth. When her body jerks I bite down harder.

"Ow!" She curses.

"Stay still," I order again.

Her nostrils flare but she holds still this time as my

tongue laps at the hardened peaks.

"Shit," she mumbles, "shit. This is wrong. So fucking wrong."

I grin against her skin, she's right about that at least.

This is where lines get blurred, goal posts get moved.

Her father is out, set to destroy my entire world and here I am, getting myself a sweet taste of his daughter.

Like the good girl I know she can be, she stays dead still, the only give away that she wants this as much as I do is the way her breathing comes out heavy, the way her eyes are hooded and pupils blown.

I run a hand up between the valley of her breasts, nails biting into the skin at her collarbones until I find her throat, still injured from the fight she put up in the apartment.

An unexpected pang of guilt tightens my chest and I find myself feathering my touch over the delicate areas, somehow wishing that the bruises would go away if I just loved them enough.

Replacing my hand with my mouth I trail kisses up her chest, scraping my teeth across her collar and she tilts her head back, allowing me access to her throat. I bite and nip at her skin, pressing hard into her flesh.

My cock presses into her lower belly, wanting in on the action.

I shove her back on the bed and she glares up at me, her eyes narrowed.

I cock my head, watching her, top half naked, breasts heaving with each chaotic breath.

I've never seen anything more beautiful. I see the war within herself, the one in which she battles on whether she wants to kill me or kiss me and I live for this shit.

"Take them off," I refer to the sweats.

"No."

"Are you going to deprive yourself of this?" I ask.

"Are you?" She taunts.

I grin.

"Take them off, little bird."

Grumbling, she hooks her fingers into the waist band and tugs them down her thighs, shoving them with zero grace.

"Happy?"

"Very."

With her bare pussy on show to me, glistening with her arousal I almost snap. Seeing her naked is one thing, seeing her naked, needy and so very ripe for the taking is a whole other story.

"Touch yourself."

"Fuck you."

She does as she is told though, her delicate fingers working over her flat stomach and then dipping between her legs, smearing her wetness over the folds until she finds the little bundle of nerves at the top. Her head rolls back as she rubs her clit, eyes fluttering closed.

"Look at me." I bark, palming my cock through the material of my pants.

Her eyes ping open and she levels me with a look that would flail a weaker man.

Her jaw twitches as her body tenses up, ready for her orgasm.

"Stop." I order.

"What?"

"Stop!"

Her hand stops moving but she doesn't come away from her core. I press forward, snatching her hand away.

"You're a fucking asshole," she grumbles.

I bury my face between her legs, licking her from her hole all the way to the top and she crashes down on the bed, her hips lifting, wanting more. I flick my tongue against her clit, sliding a hand up until it presses against the entrance.

"Your pussy is so fucking sweet," I growl against her flesh, lapping at her, tasting her arousal on my tongue.

I slide a second finger in.

"So tight, little bird."

"Shut up."

I pump her with my fingers whilst I toy with her clit, sucking it into my mouth, nipping at it with my teeth.

"Oh fuck!" She moans.

"Come for me," I demand.

I curl my fingers inside, finding the rough patch on her internal walls and she comes undone. "That's it, little bird, all over my tongue, I want to taste it." Her thighs clamp around my head, her hips grind on my face and I continue to lick her, tasting it, feeling it with every spasm and roll of her hips.

"Yes, oh fuck, yes!" She screams.

When her pussy calms I pry her thighs apart and come up for air, leaving her arousal all over my face. Her eyes narrow when I go to the first button of my shirt.

She watches with intense focus as I flick through each one and then slide the shirt off my shoulders. Her eyes roam over every inch of me, eyes snagging on the scars that litter my abdomen. The stab wound beneath the ribs, the lacerations across my stomach, the bullet hole in my shoulder. Let's not forget about the fresh one in my arm, courtesy of this little siren.

I flick the button on my pants and shove them and my boxers down to the floor. My cock bobs in front of me, hard and ready.

She swallows.

I jerk my hand up the shaft, smearing the precum over the crown.

"Are you ready, little bird?"

11

Wren

This is insanity.

This is going to kill me.

And yet, I'm shameless as I peruse his entire body. All the hard lines, the ruthless edges, the sharp corners. He's as hard as stone, all his muscles defined, peaks and ridges, rolling muscles and valleys. His defined abdomen is riddled with scars, some easily identified as bullets, others not so much but it doesn't take away from the appeal of the man. His waist tapers into a V, forming an arrow down to his hard, proud cock that juts out from his hips. Muscular thighs, one still bandaged with a white gauze where I stabbed him.

I grin a little at that.

He steps towards me, his jaw clamped tight.

"Open your legs."

I comply but scowl in his direction, making sure he knows I'm not happy obliging to his demands. I just want him. I need him to settle this ache in me, the one that has been present since I first laid eyes on him. The man is poison and antidote all the same.

Once won't hurt then I can go back to hating him and plotting my escape.

He kneels on the bed, coming towards me.

"This isn't going to be sweet," he warns. "I *am* going to *fuck* you."

"Then do it already," I snap.

He quirks a brow and grabs an ankle, pulling me towards him where he then settles between my legs.

"You have quite the mouth on you," he growls, pushing his thumb between my lips. I bite him.

He hisses out a breath but doesn't withdraw his thumb, instead he pushes down on my tongue which only forces my teeth to withdraw from his flesh so he can remove his finger.

"Maybe we should put it to good use," he contemplates.

"You put your dick in my mouth and I'll bite it off." I warn.

"No returning the favor?" He smirks.

"Not to those who don't deserve it."

He nods his head back and forth and without warning, he shoves his hips forward, impaling me on his cock.

He's so big and I'm well, not, that the pain of it makes my eyes water. The invasion is all consuming, my pussy frantically pulses, a mixture of pleasure and pain as it tries to accommodate the size of him.

"Shit!" I groan.

His hand comes up to grip my throat, just below the jaw, pressing hard against the pressure points at the joint.

"Maybe I should teach you some manners," he warns, his voice all growl.

"Fuck you!"

He pistons his hips, pulling out almost all the way before slamming back in so far I'm sure he's touching something deep inside me that should never be touched.

The pain has evaporated. Gone.

He fucks me hard and relentlessly, his cock pounding me, our skin slapping together.

The grip on my throat becomes tight as he lifts himself to pound harder, pushing me further into the mattress.

"Shit," I moan.

He keeps going, pulsing his cock in and out of me, my body reacting with each wave of pleasure that shoots through me. This isn't sex. This is anger. Frustration. Rage. He fucks me with his emotions. Punishing me for crimes I did not commit. And I let him and then some.

"Such a good girl," he comments through gritted teeth.

"I hate you!"

He growls, releasing my throat as he lifts himself onto his knees and yanks my hips up. In this position he goes deeper, rubbing up against that sweet spot inside me that has me seeing stars.

"Are you going to come for me?" He asks through gritted teeth.

"I'm going to come for *me.*"

He chuckles. Taking away one hand from my hip to press his thumb against my clit.

"Yes!" I scream. He presses harder and I'm gone. My walls clamp around him as the orgasm grips me with everything it has. My muscles coil tight, my spine straightens and I cry out. I fall off the edge with no parachute and fall into the darkness below. And I allow it. I take it. I want it.

His own release comes seconds later and I watch him, through hooded eyes I see when it happens. His jaw clamps tight, the corded muscle in his neck becomes unbelievably taut, like it'll snap at any moment and his hips still, his cock jerking wildly inside me as he empties himself.

"Fuck!" He roars.

Spent and breathing heavy he falls on top of me, holding his weight on his elbows. My eyes close as regret churns almost instantly, making my stomach roll. There's no denying how much I wanted him, how much I still want him but the guilt of doing it, having it, it wars with the desire. I feel ashamed. Stupid.

I shove him off me, using my hands to cover myself. I feel his eyes watching me, it burns everywhere they touch but I can't face him.

For the first time since being here I feel uncontrollable tears sting my eyes, emotion clogging my throat and making my nose sting. I tilt my face away, trying to regain composure but I can't stop it this time.

The first tear slips down my cheek but clearly, I haven't been successful in my attempt to hide from him.

He pinches my chin and turns my face towards him before the rough pad of his thumb swipes away the fat tear. Shock has my eyes bouncing to his face but he's not watching me, he's looking at the droplet of water on his thumb as if he's never seen tears before, never witnessed sadness, regret or pain.

The tear rolls down his thumb and eventually he drags his eyes away from that to look at my face. His silver eyes bounce between mine, a frown dragging at his brows then simply sucks his thumb into his mouth, tasting my regret on his tongue. Without another word, he collects his belongings and struts, naked from the room, closing the door loudly on the way out.

I break.

For the first time since he kidnapped me at gunpoint, I fucking break hard.

I've always been good at keeping my emotions in check, deep breathing exercises, yoga, meditation but this unrelenting turmoil makes me want to scream.

I snatch my clothes from where they've been discarded

106

and shove them on, wincing when I feel him seeping onto the insides of my thighs. Just fucking perfect that is. He didn't even wear a condom. Jesus Christ.

Granted I was on birth control, but I hadn't taken it in days, not since they took me, and I doubted he had any diseases, but I wasn't the girl who got so worked up she forgot to use protection. I doubted this one time will cause a pregnancy, but this shit happens all the time.

Who am I kidding? I'm not going to live long enough to worry about being knocked up.

I walk towards one of the doors in the room and open it, finding a huge walk in closet but it's empty, not even a single box here. Closing that I head to the next and sigh in relief, finding a small en-suite. No shower or tub but there is a toilet with a basin over a small white cupboard. I quickly clean myself up, discarding the sweats I'd only just put on for a pair of fresh leggings I spotted in the drawers earlier. No underwear but beggars can't be choosers.

My eyes sting as I head over to the one window in the room. The sun is setting now, the sky turning a fiery orange as the sun lowers in the sky, sitting on the horizon. Shadows stretch across the pristine lawn. The entire house is surrounded by a ten foot wall and from this room I can't see where you enter or leave. Beyond the wall, trees surround the compound, thick and dark, the canopies lush and full. Birds dart between the branches, disappearing into the woods. We must be a decent way out the city, as far as I know there are no thick wooded areas until you start hitting the outskirts of the city centre. If we're even in the city at all.

I rejudge the drop from the window. There's absolutely zero way I'd walk away from a jump this high without some serious damage and he knows it, which is probably why I'm in this particular room.

I head to the door and pull the handle but of course it's locked, why wouldn't it be?

What else is there to do but go to sleep? Fatigue makes my limbs sluggish and lazy so I crawl up the bed, burying myself into the downy pillows. A nap will do me some good. It'll help clear the sex haze Alexander left me in and then I can figure my shit out.

My lids close heavily and it's not long before the claws of sleep drag me under.

12

Lex

I fill the glass for the third time, not bothering to stop at just a couple of fingers like I had the first two times. What's the point? I'm just going to drink it too quick and have to repeat this process in a few moments anyway.

The house is eerily quiet, too quiet though I'm far from alone.

A couple of men are stationed through the house, they know better than to make their presence known, especially when I'm in this particular mood.

I stare at the smashed mirror on the other side of the room and then down at my split knuckles. There are still shards of glass inside the wounds, I couldn't get them all out so I may as well let them fester.

That was a stupid mistake. Fucking her, feeling her… seeing her cry.

I can still smell her on my skin, taste her on my tongue.

Sweet, sweet little bird.

I take a healthy sip of the whiskey, feeling it burn down my throat, warming that desolate place inside of me.

But it's not so desolate now, is it? No, that would be simple. That would make this whole thing easy but when has my life ever been easy?

Never is the answer to that.

I was young, too young really when my father introduced me to the evil of this world and this life. At ten, I witnessed him kill a man. At twelve, I stood by as his men tortured and beat the living shit out of another. At sixteen, he put the gun in my hand.

"If you want power, son, you have to take it. This life is cruel and dark and the only way men like us make it is if we become just as cruel and just as dark."

"What did he do?" I asked, looking at the grown man on his knees in front of me. His face was covered in dirt and blood, one eye was swollen shut, his bottom lip split and still seeping fresh blood over his wet chin. The blood and the tears mingled together, causing it to run faster and drip from the tip of his chin. He looked broken. So very broken.

I knew what my father was. I was *proud* of him. I vowed to be just like him. I would take the power. I would hold this city in the palm of my hand and I would control it all. He was right, in this life nothing comes easy. Nothing is given and if you let it, it'll all slip away, and you'll be left to rot in a ditch of your own making.

There will be those who will want what you have, those

who will use force to take it from you, the enemies will be vast and plentiful, each one worse than the last but you had to be bigger, better.

"He stole from us." My father said, *"He tried to take something that did not belong to him. He was given trust and he used it. For that, we do not forgive. We show no mercy."*

"When do we show mercy?" I had asked.

My father stepped towards me, he gripped my wrist and forced me to level the gun with the man's head.

"Mercy is something no one can tell you to give. Despite what many believe, we are not evil. We feel and we hurt like everyone else, we may straddle the line between right and wrong but what is power without consequence? When you rule this city you will understand that mercy will come to those who deserve it."

"And this man doesn't deserve it," I concluded. Because he didn't. He may have worked for the family for a few years, he was even trusted but he broke that trust and every action, good or bad has a consequence. To keep power you have to prove your worth. If I didn't pull that trigger and I gave him mercy, people could see me as weak. As the Silver too compassionate to do a damn thing about a thief.

I still remember the way the trigger compressed under my finger, the loud bang that echoed around the small room. It made my ears ring. Blood splattered up the wall as the bullet pierced through his skin and then his skull.

I threw up after that. My father patted me on the back

and told me he was proud. It was only few weeks after that that I did it again and then again until killing became something of a chore. When I ended a life now, I felt nothing because the people dying deserved it in one way or another.

This life isn't for the faint of heart, you come into it knowing that your life could be cut short in a matter of seconds but we continue anyway because the rewards are just as great.

The Silver's have run the City of Brookeshill for generations and for generations to come it'll only be the Silver name that rule these streets.

Killing Wren Valentine gives everyone the same lesson. Try to take what's mine and you'll feel my wrath. And I would do anything and use anyone to make sure they knew it.

When Wren is dead, when her father has felt the pain, then I'll do what is needed. I'll kill the man. Slowly. Painfully. Unforgiving.

This is *my* city and I'll be dead before it goes anywhere else.

I know what I have to do. I know it and yet here I am, a busted hand, half way to drunk because the girl has got in my head.

This shit doesn't happen to me.

I'm Alexander fucking Silver. I'm fucking king!

Valentine kept his promise. It's been three days and Wren has not been safely deposited back in his hands. He burned down two more of my locations. Luckily, I had everything moved into new warehouses and buildings that only a few on my payroll know about meaning his arson was pointless.

He thinks he can hurt me but he clearly doesn't know me. I'm three steps ahead of him.

I sit on the plush sofa on the balcony overlooking the dance floor of the club. Revelers grind and pulse to the fast beat of the music. The scent of sex and sweat permeates the air. A girl, dressed scantily in a red dress slides onto my lap. My hand goes to her hip and I roll my head to the side to look at her.

"Hi," she smiles. Plump red painted lips pull back to show pearly white teeth and her eyes flash with desire. Blonde hair spills over one shoulder, the ends tickling her breasts that threaten to spill from the satin of her dress.

I cock my head and narrow my eyes. If only her hair was darker, redder, her eyes green, mouth pink…

Shit.

I push the girl from my lap and lean forward on a growl. With a scathing look the girl prances away to find another man willing to play her games. I've avoided going into Wren's room since I fucked her, unsure if I'd be able to control myself now that I'd had a taste.

"Why haven't you done it yet?" Ryker asks next to me as if sensing where my thoughts have taken me, tipping his whiskey back. His voice is low so the other guys around us don't hear but I still shoot him a look. If he were anyone else, I'd have rammed a blade straight into his throat for questioning me.

"It isn't time."

It's a lie. I should have killed her days ago and dumped her body for daddy to find and yet she's still sitting pretty in my compound.

I needed to send him the message that I wasn't to be fucked with but then how am I to do that if I'm avoiding the girl like a fucking pussy.

I could send someone else to do it, I almost did on a couple of occasions but then I changed my mind, telling myself I had to be the one. I had to be the one to level that gun to her head and pull the trigger, I had to be the one to witness the life draining from her. She was a Valentine, and they were fucking parasites. They had come into my city and tried to take over, but this host wasn't willing. No, it would be me to take out the Valentine's. Only me.

He took away the only woman that ever mattered to me, my mother and for that I would take away the only woman that matters to him, his daughter.

It made sense.

So why the fuck wasn't she rotting in a grave by now?

My fingers tighten on the glass in my hand, so hard that the cuts over my knuckles split back open. I feel the warm blood trickle over my fingers, snaking around the digits like a crimson snake.

Ryker chuckles next to me and I swing my glare on him. I've always had a short temper but this short? No. I feel like I might explode.

"What's funny, asshole?"

He shakes his head, "Someone has a soft spot."

"Fuck you."

"Is that what she said?"

I roll my eyes, "Grow up."

He quirks a brow, "Fuck her and get it out of your system. The quicker you end this the quicker we can all move forward. There are deals on the table that you're ignoring."

"What deals?"

"Sanchez has been with the Mexicans, they want to move Coke into the city, real good shit according to him but the Mexicans know they need to come to you."

"Dawson won't like it," I comment.

"Dawson can grow a pair."

I shake my head. The Dawson family has been working with the Silver's almost as long as we've had this city. It would be wrong of me to consider a new drug route without going to the man himself. He's always managed that side of the business so it begs the question as to why Sanchez didn't go to him directly.

My brow tugs down at that train of thought. There's been a lot of shady shit going on recently that I haven't had the brain capacity to think of but now, with this on the table it's all coming to light.

"Shit," Ryker hisses, jumping to his feet as he peers down at the dance floor below.

I follow his eye line to see what's snagged his attention.

"That's Valentine's right hand," Ryker says.

"I see him."

"He's brave," Ryker growls, pulling his gun from the holster.

I grab his arm, "Really? In a crowded club? Use your fucking brain."

He rolls his eyes, "As if the cops will do shit about it."

I curl my finger to a couple of my guys and jerk my head to the guy sat at the bar. Samuel Jameson is as much a pain in my ass as his boss but why the fuck is he here?

I guess I'm about to find out.

13

Lex

Samuel jerks out of my guys hold and smooths his hands over the lapels of his suit jacket. His dark hair is speckled with silver, and he looks years older than when I last saw him a mere few months ago.

"Times hard?" I kick my leg up, resting my ankle on my knee as I tip my whiskey back, "You look like shit."

"Fuck you, Silver."

I chuckle, "Touchy."

His eyes dart around, not at my men even though it should be them he's worried about. No he looks everywhere else, at the cameras installed all around the club, at the dancers below, the bar. He doesn't seem to care much for the guns trained on him at all. I don't comment, instead choosing to keep that information to myself.

He looks nervous as all hell, jumpy, paranoid and something tells me it isn't because he's just entered the lion's den all by himself.

"Valentine send you?"

He nods once.

"Interesting," I say, "couldn't get the balls to do it himself?"

"He knows you'd put a bullet in his head quicker than he could speak, or am I wrong?"

"You're not wrong," the man is in hiding. Has been since the day he murdered my mother because he knows how this will end and he's only delaying the inevitable.

Ryker squeezes his shoulder and lowers him forcefully into the sofa opposite me. He was stripped of his weapons the moment my guys got a hold of him, but he didn't try to run which is how I know he's here to relay a message.

Brave. Neither Valentine nor Jameson could know whether I would let him leave here alive.

I'm still debating it myself. I pull the gun from its holster and hold it in my lap, carelessly stroking my fingers over the smooth surface, caressing the trigger like one might a lover.

His eyes glance down at the weapon and then back up to me, "You don't want to hear what he has to say?"

"Not particularly but humor me anyway."

"He wants to set up a meeting." Jameson swallows, "a trade."

118

"A trade?" I'm not even remotely interested. There isn't a single thing Valentine has that I could want.

"He'll leave the city in exchange for his daughter."

I laugh, "You honestly expect me to believe that?"

"Believe what you want, he's just a father who wants his girl back."

"Wren isn't his girl," I growl, "in fact, has she ever been? He sent her off to live with Benjamin Lawson, pretended that he wasn't even her father."

"That was for her own protection."

"No, if it were for her protection then he would have sent her far, far away. To a family not even linked to this city or this life, he kept her close for one reason."

"What reason is that?"

"He wants her in eventually, to take over from him one day."

Samuel doesn't answer but he grimaces which tells me he doesn't believe that to be true. But what else could he want Wren for?

"You're making a mistake, Silver."

"Am I?"

"Yes," Samuel growls, "You have no idea what you're playing with."

"Oh I think I do," I say to him, "this is my city, it's you who have tried to come in and take it, and it's you who's going to fucking lose it all, starting with the girl."

"So you'll kill a completely innocent woman in the name of revenge?"

"Yes."

"You're making a mistake, this is bigger than you. You'd be wise to surrender."

"I'll be dead before I give up this City."

"Trust me," Samuel stands, "it won't be long before you join all those you've buried yourself."

I level the gun with his chest, "You can send a message back to Valentine that his daughter will be dead in less than twenty-four hours. He best make his peace because he's next."

Samuel shakes his head and then turns his back on me, heading to the elevators to take him back down.

"Oh and Jameson?" I call out.

He stops, back stiffening, "I see you in my club again I'll decorate the walls with your brain."

A couple of my guys see him down and Ryker takes the empty chair.

"What do you think he meant this shit is bigger than us?"

I shrug, "It's a bluff. Valentine knows he can't win so he'll use anything."

"I don't know," Ryker shakes his head, "Something

doesn't feel right."

"Just keep an ear to the ground, report back if anything raises your suspicions."

"So this is it then?" Ryker asks as I stand and tip back the remainder of my drink, "You're gonna finally say farewell to your little house guest?"

I nod once and head out.

As much as my cock liked the girl it's time I wring that little birdy's neck.

As always, the downstairs section of the club is rammed, familiar faces swim in the chaos of people, naked girls grind on laps and dance on the poles, and I watch as people who pretend to have the authority in this city lean down and snort their money up their noses. There's white dust on damn near every surface and more money than sense being stuffed into the panties of the girls I employ here.

I tip my head to the chief of police, noting the security camera trained right on him as he snorts a line of coke off the stomach of one of my girls.

That'll be a nice little bribe should I need it.

Outside, the air is humid, the promise of a storm pressing in. Angry dark clouds roll through the sky, suffocating the moon and stars.

My driver waits for me at the curb and I slide into the back, finally taking a breath.

It'll be twenty minutes before I hit the compound, so I settle back and close my eyes.

This will be the only time I get peace, here in the back of the Mercedes. The windows are heavily tinted, the engine smooth and quiet as it rolls through the streets of Brookeshill.

The partition between the back and front seats is up and I can pretend, just for a moment that all this shit isn't happening.

I don't remember a time in my life where anything was easy. Don't get me wrong, my transactions were smooth, my business dealings successful but there's always something. Like a shadow, you can't get rid of the shit that comes with running this city, it'll always follow, even in the darkness, you're never quite alone.

We're turning down Commercial Avenue when the back windscreen shatters.

"Fuck!"

I duck low, pulling my gun but the fire is heavy and quick. A bullet pierces the partition ahead of me, right where my drivers head would be and the car careens to the side before slamming into a street light. My body slams forward, hitting the seats in front of me, my head colliding with the side of the car. The fire continues, pouring shards of glass down on me. It feels as if it's from all sides but I know it's only on the left side so I use that to my advantage and slide out the right, keeping my head low and ignoring the way my body protests at the movements.

I peer around the edge of the car finding two motorcycles, their riders pointing machine guns at the car. The smell of gas hits my nose. Shit, they've pierced the tank, any minute now it's going to go up in flames.

I realize quickly the guys are low lives, belonging no doubt to one of the small gangs that keep popping up on the south side of the city. Valentine probably has them on his payroll.

I check the ammo in my gun and figure out the best way to take them out without having my own head blown off in the process. If they were my guys they would have stationed themselves on both sides of the vehicle to ensure nobody could escape but that's what you get for hiring idiots. Valentine isn't a smart man after all.

Eventually the bullets stop flying and I peer around the corner, finding the riders jerking the handle bars of their bikes to the left before twisting the throttle and speeding away.

Fuck.

With a sigh, I stand from my position and check through the window. My driver stares lifelessly towards me, the front windscreen red with his blood.

Again, if they were part of my crew, they would have checked the target was dead before hitting the road.

The only way they could have figured out I was alone was intel. Samuel saw me leave and called it in.

The fucker. That's why he was here. Not to relay some bullshit message but to check my whereabouts, my movements. I should have known.

I should have figured that shit out! I didn't get as far as I have got by being stupid and there's only one person to blame for this distraction.

Wren fucking Valentine.

14

Wren

I hear the door slam loudly. Considering how quiet the house is and has been for the past three days I can only assume who ever just entered is pissed or is, in fact, a bear.

I climb from the bed, I don't know how I know but I know that whoever it is, they are coming for me. My nerves light up, adrenaline pumps through my system, coiling my muscles. I might die here but there is no damn way in hell I'm going out without a fight. I'll be sure to do damage where I can.

I'm ready when the lock on my bedroom door disengages and the mammoth of the man that is Alexander, storms into the room.

He is covered in blood, there's a cut on his brow that is leaking red liquid down the side of his face, bruising has already started to shadow his jawline and partially down the side of his neck. Damn, he looks like he got hit by a truck.

I spot the gun he has levelled at me, not at my head though, my chest but he isn't pulling the trigger despite the murderous glint in his steely eyes.

I rush him, if he were going to shoot me, he would have done it by now, either that or I have death wish. The gun doesn't go off as my shoulder slams into his abdomen. I won't lie, it feels like I just charged into a brick wall though he does stagger a bit from the impact. A grunt leaves his mouth but he's quick to wrap his arms around my middle, pushing back with his own weight which is considerably more than mine. The man is a tank, a broad-shouldered wall of pure muscle and violence though size isn't everything in a fight. I'm lithe, elegant even, I move quickly and don't think for a minute that my size gives me a weak punch.

I slide out of his grip and wrap my fingers around his wrist, twisting it until his elbow threatens to snap.

The gun clatters to the floor and I kick it away, watching where is slides so I can grab it for later use.

I'm using his weakness right now, the fact that he's clearly taken a beating before coming here is my advantage even if a tiny piece of me is worried about his injuries. I mean how fucked up is that? The guy kidnaps me, fucks me and then leaves for three days. Whenever I asked where he was, I got grunts and growls in response, that seems to be the native language amongst the fuckers Alexander employs.

He snatches out of my grip and shoves me hard enough that I stumble back onto the bed. He advances like a lion stalking a gazelle, eyes watching every movement, every flinch and twitch. I roll from the bed until it's the only thing that separates us.

His shoulders heave and his eyes narrow.

"Should have pulled the trigger," I taunt.

His brow twitches, "You're right, I should have."

"Why'd you hesitate, huh?"

"Perhaps I wanted to give you a head start. Maybe I wanted to watch you run. Wanted to see how far you could get before I eventually caught you."

I scoff, "Of course you did."

I don't miss the heated gaze he throws my way, I don't miss the way his pupils dilate and his jaw clenches as his eyes roam down my body. I'm back in my sleep shorts now that they've been washed and a small sports bra after getting too warm in here the night before. I wouldn't sleep naked, but this was enough to keep me cool.

He wants me. Even when he wants to kill me, he lusts after me, I just don't know which one he wants more.

It's terrifying and exhilarating all the same.

I should probably get my head checked.

My eyes track to the door, he's left it wide open, probably not expecting such a push back. He grins, with his bloodied face and the violence shining in his eyes, he looks manic and sexy as fuck.

Just get out, I tell myself, we can admire him from afar.

Preferably far, far away.

I have speed on my side, but did I really think I could make it? Only one way to find out. I sprint for the exit, weaving past the furniture and it's right there, freedom so close I can taste it, but a thick arm bands around my waist and I'm tugged back hard enough the wind is knocked out my lungs as I collide with his chest. His breath comes out heavy as he pants next to my ear, causing the curls around my face to tickle against my skin. The warm scent of whiskey clings to him but there's other smells on him too, gasoline, smoke though I can't focus on that too much as he presses me up against the wall, his chest to my back. I feel his hardness resting on my spine and memories of the last time we were here flash in my mind.

Warmth floods me.

"What is it about you, hm?" He growls, pushing his cock harder into me, "that gets me harder than a fucking rock every time."

I don't mean to, but I moan, a slight whimper that puffs from my lips.

"You're fucking batshit, that's why," I breathe.

"I fear you like this kind of crazy little bird."

Yes, "No."

His hand comes up to cup the back of my neck, holding me against the wall whilst his other slips away from my body, coming back a moment later. Something sharp is pressed against my rib cage, enough that it bites into my skin but doesn't cut.

The mix of adrenaline, fear and desire causes my sex to clench, a wash of lust and heat running wild through my body. I can't think straight, only feel. And I feel everything. Every puff of breath, every twitch of his finger on my neck, the way his hard shaft digs into my back.

"What will you do?" I ask.

"What I want and what I need are two very different things."

He slides the blade down my body, stopping at the waistband of my shorts.

"So which one will win?"

I'm helpless right now, he has the upper hand with this position and the knife and I'm glad my logical sense is still working, even if it is sluggish and constricted beneath the haze.

"I don't know," he admits and for the first time I sense his reluctance here. Something or someone is telling him he has to end me but that's not what he wants.

I push back against him and he groans, the tip of the blade presses a little harder into my skin. It'll cut if I'm not careful.

His lips find my throat and presses a gentle kiss there before his teeth sink into my flesh hard. He licks the string immediately before doing it again and again, with each scrape of his teeth comes the soothing caress of his tongue and it works like a damn charm. My insides have knotted so tight I'm not sure I'll ever come undone on my own. It needs to be him. With each pass of his mouth that blade digs in just a little more.

"Fuck," I growl, pushing back, "touch me damn it."

He spins me suddenly and presses me back against the wall, the blade poised in front of him. My chest heaves as I watch him step forward, positioning the sharp edge at the hem of one leg. A quick slice and the fabric opens, he does the same on the other side and I feel rather than watch the thin cotton fall to the floor at my feet. I'm bare to him completely, in just my sports bra which he gets rid of just a moment later in the same fashion.

"You're so perfect, little bird," he coos, eyes roaming over every inch of exposed skin. "So pretty."

His heated stare burns me from the inside out and in the silence the regret of giving him this, this power, starts to churn my insides. With him distracted, I lunge for the blade held loosely in his hand and snatch it away.

I hold it out in front of me, pressing the tip into his abdomen enough that I see blood begin to bloom on his white shirt.

His eyes finally drop from my naked body down to the blade as if only just realizing I have it now.

"Do it, little bird," he breathes, daring to lift his hands to trace the outline of my body, fingers spread, his palms a whisper away from my skin. Even his phantom touch makes goose bumps chase across my skin.

"Stop calling me that."

Hearing that name, the one he's been calling me for days now gives me a fluttery sort of feeling in my stomach and I hate it. I don't want to feel anything for this man. I want nothing from him.

But I want everything.

"Do it," he presses, leaning into the blade, dropping his hands.

Shit.

This is it. I could stab him and make a run for it, granted I'd be as naked as the day I was born but I'd be free.

And yet, I can't fucking do it.

I can't do it!

His nostrils flare as his eyes level with mine, there is no fear of death in his eyes, just a sense of acceptance. I fucking hate it. I hate it all!

A loud cry leaves me as my fingers open, dropping the knife to the hardwood floor. It clatters loudly in the deafening silence.

And then he's on me, his tongue pushing between my lips, his cock grinding into my pussy as if he's starved and the only thing that will sustain him is my body. He lifts me, slamming my back into the wall as my legs go around his hips. In this position the bulge in his pants presses to my swollen clit. Blood and dirt smears against my skin, the grit on him scratching against my skin, rubbing off onto me from him but I don't care. His kiss claims me, it kills me and brings me back all in the same breath and I let it because I'm weak. Fucking weak.

Pleasure builds in my core with the grind of his hips against my centre and my nails claw at his back, drawing even more blood from him.

"I can't do it," he pants against my skin, "I can't hurt you."

"*Please*," I whimper when he pulls away.

Hands and fingers pull at his belt and buttons and then he's entering me in one swift movement. His cock fills me until all I can feel is him, pressing into me hard and everything else, all that I was before melts away.

15

Lex

She is my weakness. *Mine.*

Despite all that is fucked in this world, this woman belongs to me.

I piston my hips, fucking her hard against the wall. Her cries and pleas like damn music to my ears. She feels so damn good, her tight pussy like a vice around my cock, taking everything from me, all that I have to give, she takes and gives back. The loud slap of our skin echoes in the room, her nails dig into my shoulders as my tongue punches between her lips, mimicking what my cock is doing.

Her legs tighten around my hips, a sign she's almost there so I stop.

"What are you doing!?" She screeches.

I can't help it, I grin as I pull her from the wall, my dick still buried in her core and walk her to the bed, dropping her ungraciously to the mattress. The ache of the car crash is long gone, replaced with the burning need to lose myself in the girl in front of me. The enemy no less and yet I'm addicted. I need her as badly as I need air to breathe.

I kick out the rest of my clothes, taking great pleasure in the way her eyes follow the lines of my body.

"You're hurt," she breathes, watching me kneel between her legs and line myself up with her entrance.

"Do you care, little bird?"

Her eyes narrow but then widen as I slam back inside of her, gripping her hips until her ass levitates off the bed. A tingle rushes down my spine as my climax builds and I drop her hips, leaning forward until I have her throat in my hands.

"Are you going to come, little bird?" I growl, my hips jerking chaotically. Her whole body moves when I slam into her and her back arches off the bed, her breasts heaving. Her climax comes quickly, her core spasming and tightening around my cock, forcing my own orgasm to barrel through me.

I come with a roar, collapsing down onto her slim frame but managing to hold most of my weight off her. Her breath comes out in quick rough puffs against the shell of my ear, and I don't know if she realizes she's doing it, but her fingers feather lightly up my rib cage, a touch so gentle and soft I wonder if it's actually there. It's a complete contrast to the way we are, the push and the pull, the fight and the violence, this is something in between that, something dangerous.

I have had every opportunity, every chance to do what

is needed but I can't. I've never hesitated, never questioned it, regardless of situation, if it needs to be done, I've done it and yet I can't hurt her. I can't destroy her.

"So what now?" She breathes softly.

"You're mine," I pull out of her, wincing at the loss of the tightness around me, "Just because I'm showing you mercy doesn't mean you're free."

Her brow arches, "You don't own me."

"That's where you're wrong little bird," I tug my pants back on, wincing with the pain in my body now that the adrenaline and the lust has seeped from my veins, "You belong to me now. All that you were and all that you are is *mine.*"

I come down just as Ryker is storming into the house, a frantic look on his face.

"What the fuck happened!?" He hollers, no doubt referring to the car and the shit I left behind. I called it in of course but then I grabbed one of my guys to bring me here. I don't even know where the guy went after I came in here like a raging bull ready to destroy everything in its path.

"Valentine put out a hit," I say calmly.

"You need to get rid of the girl," Ryker growls, "this is becoming more hassle than it's worth."

"I've made a decision," my voice is calm, steady, the anger roaring in my veins only an hour or so ago gone now. I'll have my vengeance, but it'll be in a different form. "I'm keeping her."

"She's not a pet," Ryker huffs, "put her out her damn misery."

"I don't pay you to have an opinion," I warn.

"I'll fucking do it myself."

"Touch her and I'll fucking kill you," I snarl.

He stops in his tracks, his body stiffening.

"Friend or not Ryker, you answer to me!" I bellow, "and I will cut you down just as quickly as I put you up. Touch the girl and I will not hesitate to put a bullet in your fucking skull. Do you hear me?"

He shakes his head, "Loud and clear."

"Get the fuck out," I roar, "get out!"

Ryker turns to me, his eyes searching my face but then he sighs, stepping up to me. I resist the urge to pound into his face when his hand slaps down onto my shoulder, "Let me know your next move."

With that, he takes his leave. Ryker would do it, he would do what I haven't been able to and if it were anyone else, if it wasn't her, I would have let him. But she, she's like a drug, addictive and dangerous. You know you shouldn't take a hit, but you do it anyway because the euphoria is too damn good to resist.

I hear her shuffling around upstairs, her steps hesitant. I left the door open, gave her free rein but she no doubt thinks it's a trick. The girl isn't stupid. Far from it.

With her lingering upstairs, I ensure the security system is engaged and set and give heads up to the guys I have stationed around the place. An eye is to be kept on her at all points except when she is in the room with me, she's not to leave the house but can go anywhere within these walls.

I shake my head at myself, running a hand down the front of my white shirt. I'm fucking filthy. Bloody. Bruised.

Valentine had some nerve sending those fuckers after me but the way it was handled just proves how right I've been about him this entire time. He's a little fish in a big pond, barely able to tread the water it's so deep.

A creak of a floorboard being compressed has my head turning towards the stairs. Wren moves like a scared cat, no, cat is the wrong word, she's more lioness if I were to compare her to a feline only, she's a little nervous, thrown off by the sudden freedom from her cage.

"Well hello, little bird," I grin, watching her watching me with narrowed eyes and pursed lips. She's dressed but not showered meaning my scent and my essence is still on her skin, in her body. I've never been a possessive man when it came to women, they were mere bodies used for convenience when I needed to let out some tension but with her, there was no doubt in my mind that I had to have her, mind, body, and soul. There was a tether between us now and no matter how hard she pulled there was no way I was letting it go.

She was mine.

Her eyes drift from me to where the front door is and I see it work through her head, the calculation of getting out, of getting away but before she can even step foot in that direction, one of my guys, a big fucker really, steps in front of the door, blocking the way.

"You can't run away from me," I tell her, settling onto the couch.

"So, what? You'll just keep me here?"

I shrug, "It depends."

"On what?" She snaps.

"Whether or not we can come to some kind of understanding. If I let you go your daddy is just going to get you and I can't be having that."

"What did Lawson do that was so bad that kidnapping his daughter was your only option?"

I laugh, "Lawson isn't your father."

Her eyes go wide, "You're lying."

"Unfortunately, I am not, little bird."

"I have nothing to do with whatever fucked up shit you get involved with."

"You're right but that was before, now, you've just become my most valuable possession."

"I want to hurt you," she admits on a breath.

"I know but you won't."

I tap the couch, inviting her to come sit with me. I'd entertain the thought of her hurting me, not because I thought she couldn't do it, she most definitely could, I have a bullet and stab wound still healing from her to prove that but because she won't. She can't. She's as obsessed with me as I am with her. It's unhealthy but then nothing in my life can be deemed healthy.

What's another unhealthy habit to add to the mix?

"You're so sure of that," she comments but sits like a good girl, as far as possible away from me mind you, with her elegant legs tucked beneath her and her hands clasped in her lap. She takes a deep breath and then meets my eyes, holding her chin up defiantly. "This situation isn't going to work for me."

I laugh, "There's a lot shit that isn't working for me," I shrug, "I'm learning to accept it."

She rolls her eyes.

"Shit like that will have you over my knee."

"Try it," she growls, rising to her knees, "see how that goes for you."

Damn, I love her temper.

"One day," I tell her, readjusting my hard cock, "and you'll love it."

"Fuck you."

"Perhaps another time," I stand from the couch, rolling my shoulders, "I have things to do."

"So what, you're just going to leave me here? What about giving me some damn answers!?"

"Another time."

She stares after me as I head towards the stairs, I stop at the bottom and turn back to her.

"Welcome to my twisted city, little bird, together we can be formidable."

16

Wren

I take my time in the shower.

I lather my hair with the expensive shampoo that smells like honey and smooth the foamy bubbles over my skin, careful over the bruises still healing plus the fresh ones Alexander so kindly gifted me after our last little tussle.

When I reach between my legs flashes of his body flexing atop of mine has my core pulsing. He had well and truly wormed his way under my skin. It was an itch I couldn't scratch, a damn ache that wouldn't go away no matter how hard I tried to remedy.

I suck in a breath as the pad of my finger rubs across my swollen bud, eyes fluttering closed as my mind conjures images of his thick body moving, his muscles flexing, the murderous glint in his eyes shining bright in the darkness.

Come for me, little bird.

My teeth bite into my bottom lip as the deep baritone of his voice rumbles through my body as if he's just said the words in my ear. My thighs shake as an orgasm hits me hard and unexpectedly.

This is what it has come to. Sleeping with my fucking kidnapper and masturbating in the shower over him.

I have a sickness and I fear there is no cure.

The shackles may be off for now, but I am no where near free. He's made sure of that with his goons stationed at every door, on every corner and every room. There's no way I can get past all of them though I'm sure it could be fun to try.

I dry off using one of the thick fluffy towels in the bathroom and step up to the mirror, rubbing the condensation on the glass with my hand.

A girl I hardly recognize stares back at me.

I look the same, they're my eyes and my lips, my freckles and wild copper hair but I don't feel like me.

Is it odd that I feel powerful?

The bruising on my throat is a mere shadow now, the one on my temple practically gone and my skin looks healthy considering the circumstances. I haven't seen myself in the mirror since he took me and I expected harsh shadows under my eyes, sunken skin, but I see none of that.

I dress in fresh clothes put out on the bed for me and go in search of the man himself. I ignore the men stationed throughout the large house which I now realize is a mansion, likely big enough to be a hotel should they wish to convert it.

Something tells me however, Alexander isn't into the hospitality business.

No, the type of business Mr Silver deals is dark, and gritty, violent and bloody. He's the man your mother warns you about, the one that looks like an angel but sins like the devil. He'll corrupt your soul, tempt you and tease you before ripping out your heart and feeding it to the wolves.

He didn't scare me though. Even though he should, I didn't feel an ounce of fear when I stood head to head with him. I felt equal, even if everything between the two of us was never in my favor.

I find him in a bathroom further down the hall, one on the other side of a large master bedroom but because the door is open and the mirror inside stretches from one side to the other I can see him in the reflection.

He's shirtless, his bronzed skin stained with dried blood the color of rust and cuts mar his back, chest and arms. There's still a bandage wrapped around his arm where I shot him and it's likely his leg is still wrapped but if they hurt him, he was a pro at hiding it. Even now, with the bruises and the cuts that look angry and raw, he doesn't wince or flinch, just does his business like it's a normal day.

And it probably is.

He's probably been through worse more times than he can remember, and these wounds are nothing but an inconvenience.

I step onto the plush carpet, my feet sinking into the fibers as I make my way across the room. The air in this space smells like him, dangerous, spicy, intoxicating and when I get to the bathroom, I notice the shower is running, steam bellowing out from the top of the glass cubicle.

His eyes flash silver as they meet mine in the mirror.

"I'm surprised you don't have a personal nurse service," I grumble.

His teeth flash as he smiles, "Care to volunteer?"

I shrug and head over to the counter, stepping in front of him and scanning over his body. His pants hang low on his narrow hips, the firm muscles of his abdomen tapering off into a V that disappears beneath the waist line. A fine dusting of hair travels from his naval and disappears under the belt but he's hairless everywhere else. The wounds on his body are superficial, grazes more than anything else but they are dirty, covered in grit or mud though the deepest and cleanest wound is on his stomach, just below his ribcage. It's clotted and the blood that had run from it has dried so I start there, taking the cotton pad from his fingers and tipping some fresh antiseptic onto the pad. I slide it over his skin, wiping away the blood before getting to the cut itself.

I didn't go deep, just enough to cause a small incision and the skin has already started to knit together. When that's clean I move to the other grazes, cleaning them up, changing the pad and reapplying the antiseptic with each new cut I find.

He stands perfectly still, the only way I can tell he's even alive is by the steady rise and fall of his broad chest. I move around his body, cleaning up as I go and start on his back. There's new and old scars all over him, some aged and silver, others still angry, raw and pink. These scars tell a story of a life lived violently.

"I should check that," I tell him, referring to the bandage on his arm.

"Want to check out your handiwork?"

"Something like that."

He holds his arm out to me and I begin to unravel the white gauze. When I pull it away I inspect the injury I caused. It wasn't a through and through, just hit him at the edge though it's deep. It looks healed enough and someone had given him stitches, they were clean too.

"You should leave this off for a while," I tell him.

He dips his chin in a nod, eyes looking down on me.

I take a fresh pad and jump up onto the counter, leaning forward so I can do the cut on his forehead and cheek. When I struggle to reach, he forces my legs apart and steps between them, his hands coming down to rest on top of my thighs. Almost absentmindedly his large hands squeeze into the soft flesh of my thighs, his fingers indenting into my skin.

A few hours ago he wanted to kill me – again – and now he's looking at me like he wants to devour me – *again*.

I ignore the heat in his gaze, I ignore the rampant desire to shove his pants down and let him take me right here on the bathroom counter. That last time was the last time. It can't happen again.

The lines have already been blurred and crossed two too many times, I can't let it continue to destroy me.

"You're good now," I whisper.

"I've never been good, Wren." He sighs, stepping from between my legs and turning to the shower.

I don't look away when he shoves out of his clothes and pulls on the door to step inside. I don't even look away when he turns to me, his cock clearly on show through the glass. Watching is different than doing, right? Right. So whilst I might not allow myself to sleep with him again, I can watch.

And there's no denying I'll enjoy it too.

I watch him work the soap into a lather, smoothing the foam across his muscles, rubbing away any remaining dried blood on his skin. There're bruises now forming from whatever happened earlier.

"So are you going to fill me in on anything or is my presence here always going to remain a mystery?"

"Anyone ever tell you how very sharp your tongue is?"

"My trainer," I shrug, "answer the question."

"You're really quite demanding for someone who isn't calling the shots."

"Don't test me, Alexander."

His smirk is smug and infuriating, "Unfortunately Little bird, you're just a pawn."

"For what?"

"Your father crossed the wrong family, it's time he learned his lesson."

"So why draw it out?" I growl, jumping off the counter to stand in front of him. The glass separates us, but I still feel the power radiating off him, the way he stares, fixated on my face. His confidence is paramount to anything I've ever felt, the promise of pain and retribution is as clear as my own reflection. He wants to make my father hurt and he's using me to do it.

"I told you I wouldn't hurt you."

"And you expect me to believe a man like you?"

The shower shuts off and he steps out, leaning across to grab a towel. His muscles roll and flex with the movements as he hooks the white cotton around his hips. Water droplets roll through the crevices between his abdominal muscles, licking at his skin, clinging there as if they couldn't bear to be parted. Water clings to the long dark lashes framing his silver eyes and the muscle in his jaw jumps.

"I am a lot of things, Wren but a liar isn't one of them. What could I gain from lying to you?"

I think about that. The air in the bathroom is hot and stifling, perspiration dots across the nape of my neck so I turn and head into what I am now assuming is his bedroom. I take a seat on his bed, crossing my legs, trying like hell to ignore the scent of him that wafted up from the sheets when I sat down. The mattress is plush, soft, yielding to my weight and welcoming me, so snug and tight I could roll up and sleep.

"Well, you've made it clear that my family has

somehow wronged yours and now you're using me to get your revenge, right?"

Just saying that out loud makes me feel like I've just stepped into some sort of thriller movie or book but whatever, I've always known the world is a cruel dark place, whether I expected to witness it myself however is a different matter.

"How do I know you won't just make me trust you and then pull the rug out from under me?"

Alexander saunters to his drawers, pulling the top one open and sliding out a pair of sweats. Huh. I'd pegged him as a guy who only donned designer and perfectly tailored suits.

Before he utters a single word he drops the towel concealing himself. I avert my eyes before my brain short circuits whilst he tugs on his sweats.

"You'll be wise to follow your instincts little bird, I'm not to be trusted but right now, we both win."

"How so?"

"You get to live…" He shrugs as if that's no big deal.

"Well gee, thanks, I hadn't realized my life was so easy to throw around."

"In this world, little bird, your life is nothing."

I swallow.

"As I was saying," his voice is bordering on impatient now, "You get to live, and I get the pleasure of seeing the pain it causes your father knowing you're on my side in this war. That pain will follow him until I put the bullet with his name on between his eyes and bury him in the ground."

"You told me Lawson wasn't my dad, say I believed you," I wasn't sure what I believed truthfully, "then who is it?"

The rims of his nostrils flare as he stares at me, "Your father is Marcus Valentine."

17

Lex

There's been a part of me that has been expecting a lie.

It's what people do. We lie. We protect ourselves. Our loved ones. Sometimes we don't even mean to do it, it just simply happens because at the time it's what we think is best.

A part of me has been expecting this whole thing to be a ruse. A thing Marcus and Wren have thought up to ensure her safety, her innocence but as I stare at her face, at the big green eyes, filled with an innocence I'll never recognize in anyone else in this world I realize I've made the right choice.

My father always told me mercy is given to those who deserve it and there is no one more deserving than Wren, despite her last name.

She has no idea who her father truly is. Having been raised by Lawson, he's been the only man she's known and whilst he's far from innocent he isn't who I am after.

After deciding her death would not come by my hand I started to think of another plan.

Regardless of the situation and my incapability to do what I need to; I knew there was another way to hurt Valentine.

He's kept his daughter safely tucked away but never too far. He's watched her, doted on her from afar, ensured her future, all in preparation to bring her into the family fold.

Granted, the family fold is built on lies and thievery but to him I'm sure it's very precious.

She was being groomed to take over from him. I was almost certain of it. But that *almost* was giving me doubts, what if I was wrong here? What if that wasn't the plan at all? If that's the case, what the fuck could he want her so badly for?

They taught her how to fight, how to hold her own, that much was clear.

I had no doubt she could take down a man twice her size, hell she could have taken me down had I eased just a little, let my guard down just enough for her slip in. She had no problems protecting herself and with the right motivations and incentives it wouldn't have taken her long to get into the swing of things.

But really, what will it look like if Valentine's daughter started fighting for their enemy?

People will question his authority, his command and power, if, after all, his own daughter could turn against him then why shouldn't they?

And once he starts to feel it slip, when he realizes he's losing it all I'll ensure he knows, in those last final moments, he has most certainly *lost it all*.

I'll keep the city, I'll keep the power, I'll have his daughter and what will he be? A rotting corpse buried six feet under.

Watching her face now, after I've given her his name, I see nothing but a blank expression.

The girl is fearless.

She simply doesn't give a fuck who I am or what I can do, she'll stand in front of me and she'll give me shit and I won't deny it, I fucking love it. I live for it.

Her push when I pull, her fight, her fucking everything...

I stalk towards her and grasp her chin, tilting her face up so she's staring me directly in the face. There's so much hate in her gaze, it burns hot but not nearly as fiery as the desire that swirls in the mix. She hates that she wants me, loathes it but there's no denying this basic instinct.

Like a moth drawn to a flame, she wants to touch, to see, to feel, despite the very real threat of pain. Of death.

She fights it. Tooth and nail but she'll learn.

She'll be the good girl I know she can be and until then, I'll keep her here. With me.

"Together, little bird, we'll bring your daddy to his knees."

"I think you're mistaken," she breathes.

"Oh no," I shake my head, leaning down to brush my lips across hers. It's soft, unlike the last kisses I gave her. This one is a promise.

A promise that she'll always belong to me now that she is in my grasp.

She seems taken aback at the gentleness. She doesn't reciprocate the kiss, her lips stay still, slightly parted and her eyes open but there's a mass of emotion there I can't wait to dissect.

"I'm very rarely wrong," I tell her, "you'll learn soon enough now, sleep, we have a busy few days."

She frowns, "You think I'll bend to you, but I won't. You don't and will never own me."

"We'll see."

She scoffs, "Asshole."

"Sleep little bird," I jerk my head to the pillows, "tomorrow is a new day."

"I'm not sleeping here."

She says this as I gently coax her down onto the bed, pushing gently until her back hits the mattress.

"I'll follow," I promise. "Wherever you go, I'll be one step right behind you."

Fatigue clings to her fibers, pulling her under. I've put her through the ringer, it's bound to have caught up by now and the promise of a plush mattress and a warm body is singing to that deep seated desire for comfort. Her body curls in on itself, in the centre of the bed, she tucks her knees to her chest and wraps her arms around them before her eyes fall closed, too heavy to fight.

"I won't let you win," she mumbles, half asleep.

Leaning over her, I tuck a single copper curl behind her ear, "Oh but little bird, I've already won."

Leaving her sleeping in my bed, I head down to my office. I've been detached from the business for too long and it's time to get back on track.

I text Ryker to meet me here in an hour, he's been on the ground whilst I've been busy with Wren so he's the perfect person to get me up to speed with what's happening out there.

I'm sat in the chair behind the desk, swirling amber liquid around a glass when my right hand walks in. He still looks pissed but he's loyal. I wasn't bluffing when I told him I'd put him down and he knows it. We may have been friends since we were kids but no one questions me. Not even him. And no one, I mean fucking no one, not even the devil himself, will threaten what belongs to me.

"Boss," He greets, lowering himself in the chair opposite me.

"I want a report," I tell him, leaning forward.

"Two shipments hit the dock tonight, our guys are on it, moving the cargo to the new warehouses. The dealers were getting a little mouthy since the last lot they were due to get went up in smoke but they've settled now."

"Which dealers?"

People are forgetting their place. Not being out and in the masses is clearly giving them the wrong idea that I won't get involved should I have to.

"Dawson is dealing with it," Ryker grumbles.

"Is he now."

Ryker nods, shoulders stiff.

"What else?"

His eyes dart to the left and that's not a good sign. He's hiding something.

"What is it?" I demand.

"Valentine's men showed up at the dock tonight, throwing threats to our guys, nothing happened but one of them mentioned something that I think we need to keep an eye on."

"Go on."

"We all know how much of a pain in the ass Valentine is, he wants his daughter back and I'm sure he'll go to whatever measure he needs to, to get her back but I don't actually think Valentine is calling the shots anymore."

I lean forward, "What do you mean?"

"The guys weren't happy to be there, they found it pointless coming after a girl and whether they meant to or not, they mentioned how the boss wouldn't be happy deviating from the plan."

"What boss?"

"They called them the Syndicate."

"So Valentine has teamed up with this organization?"

Ryker shrugs, "I think it might be wise to give her back. Settle this down for a while."

"Good job I don't pay you to think." I growl. There was no way I was giving her back. Not only is that weak as fuck and goes against everything this family has built, the girl stays by my side at all times from here on out. There was no question about it.

"Well you're not going to kill her, there's no reason to keep her."

"She's mine!"

"I feel a war coming, Lex, one that I'm not sure we're prepared for. Giving her back is the smart move here."

"Valentine is tiny, you're worried he'll destroy this?" I stretch out my arms, "this is an empire Ryker, and our army is bigger, better and stronger. We have the power. He has nothing."

"Except this Syndicate, we don't know who they are and what strings they can pull."

I roll my eyes, "Well then, let's set up a little meeting shall we? Get some information."

"When?"

I scrub a hand across my mouth, "Tomorrow night. Take him to the club."

Ryker nods and stands, "Is that all?"

"Set up a meeting with Dawson," I tell him, "for Sunday, he needs to handle his dealers better."

With another nod, Ryker steps from the room. Silence settles around me once more and my mind drifts to the girl asleep in my bed.

My legs carry me from the room quietly, up the stairs until I'm hovering above her. To look at her now you would never assume the girl is feisty as hell, it's easy to forget when she sleeps so peacefully.

Without thinking too much about it, I slip into the bed beside her, pulling the blanket up to cover us both. A soft sigh escapes her lips as she rolls towards me, tucking her face against my chest. I stiffen when her arm comes around to hold my waist, her leg thrown over both of mine like she's ivy clinging to a pole. Her breath fans against my bare chest.

This was a terrible idea. I didn't sleep with women. We don't share beds other than for fucking, we certainly don't fucking cuddle. When I try to move, her body tightens against mine to the point where I truly believe if I stood, she'd still be hanging off me.

"Fuck," I grumble as she settles in further, as if trying to climb inside of me and now I can't move.

It would be easy to throw her off, wake her and kick her out of bed but now I'm here and she's curled into me like she needs me, I can't bring myself to do it.

I'm clearly going fucking soft.

That'll change tomorrow night.

When I woke this morning Wren was gone, I had searched for her, but she had made herself scarce, if I didn't know better, I would have assumed she'd made her escape. But my men have been posted throughout the house and I had confirmation Wren had been seen last in the kitchen a little over twenty minutes ago.

I hold the fabric in my hands as I continue my search for her. The house is big but not that big, she's either literally hiding likes she's a six year old playing hide and seek or she's purposely avoiding me. I'm not the quietest of people, my size doesn't allow me to be stealthy and silent but hers does. She's likely keeping an eye out and darting off without a peep before I can catch up to her.

It's pissing me off.

As I storm down one of the halls, a rhythmic thud has my ears perking. It's coming from the gym I had installed a few months back and contains every piece of equipment you could ever need. The door is cracked and through it I see her. Her copper hair is pulled up into a pony tail, it swings like a pendulum side to side as she jabs at the bag suspended from the ceiling. Her small body moves quickly, the power she packs in her punch surprising. Sweat makes her skin shine under the lights and her eyes are laser focused on her task.

"Unless you're offering to replace the bag, I don't want to talk to you," she grunts, slamming another fist into the leather. I notice then she isn't wearing any gloves or tape, her knuckles are split, trickles of blood snaking around her fingers and dripping onto the mats under her bare feet.

"That's enough," I order.

She ignores me, slamming another fist into the bag, harder this time. Blood smears across the bag.

"Enough!" I roar. "Don't fucking push me."

Her body comes to an abrupt stop, spine stiffening but then she whips her head to me, "Or what?" she taunts.

"I'm warning you, little bird, you won't like what happens next."

"You and your idle threats," she rolls her eyes.

I snap, my temper bursts and I storm across the mat towards her. The game of cat and mouse this morning, her attitude, her taunting, I've had enough today. She growls when I grab her around the waist and throw her over my shoulder. Her skin is slick with sweat but she smells fucking amazing. She slams her fists into my back, squirming and fidgeting wildly as she tries to escape. I hold her tighter, pinning her legs to stop her from kicking me. I ignore the quizzical looks my men are giving me as I take the stairs two at a time, her body bouncing roughly on my shoulder, hard enough no doubt to wind her. When I make it to my bedroom, I throw her down onto the bed.

"You'll be wise to remember who fucking owns you!" I bellow. She gets up onto her knees and glares at me.

"You don't fucking own me, Alexander Silver," she says through gritted teeth.

Her defiance should not be a turn on, but it is. I pounce on her, pinning her beneath my much larger frame and grind my hard cock into her pussy. The warmth of her penetrates her leggings and my own trousers, wrapping around my cock as if it's her delicate little palm. Her lips part, eyes rolling back as the friction presses on her clit.

"Get off me!" She breathes though it's said with zero conviction.

"This is mine," I nip the lobe of her ear, my hands slide up her slim waist, cupping her breasts, "mine." My hands travel over every inch of her, whispering against her feverish skin, committing her every dip, curve and edge to memory. "All of you is *mine*."

"Lex," my name whispers from her lips, her back arching as I grind against her through our clothes.

"Say it, little bird."

"Fuck you!"

I chuckle, "You'll learn, until then," I climb from her, swallowing down the urge to fuck her hard. When I'm sure I can control myself, I throw the fabric I've been carrying around for the better part of an hour at her. It lands on the bed next to where she is still laying, her chest heaving with her breaths.

"Put that on."

"No."

"Little bird, you'll do as you're told. There is no

negotiation here."

Her eyes narrow but she takes the dress and slides it into her lap. At least she know what's good for her. "We leave in an hour."

I don't give her time to argue further, instead I spin and head to my walk-in, closing the doors behind me. I've been relegated to a fucking closet. By a woman.

Damn it

18

Wren

The dress slides over my skin, satin material that sits around mid thigh but has a split all the way up to the hip on one side. Basically it's a wardrobe malfunction waiting to happen. It's too tight and the split too high to get away with wearing underwear but I debate for a little while wondering how much I care about that. The real question is, how vulnerable do I want to be around Alexander?

I've left my hair down, it falls wildly around my face, silky and soft from the wash I gave it an hour ago. I'm still debating when Alexander strolls back through the door.

He had hidden himself in the walk-in for twenty minutes and once he was dressed he left me in the room alone.

He's in a pristine suit, black in colour with a white shirt tucked into his pants. The top three buttons have been left undone, showing the hard expanse of bronzed skin. He's trimmed the hair around his mouth and slicked his dark hair back though a tendril still falls forward across his forehead.

His eyes devour me, taking in the high slit in the skirt and the way the material hugs my curves.

"You look beautiful."

My brows shoot up. I wasn't expecting a compliment, so much so I can't control the blush that steals its way up my cheeks. Fuck.

I hate that he affects me in anyway but mostly, I hate that I can't control my body's reaction to him. It wants him, despite my better judgement, I react and I lose control.

"I had someone collect your belongings from your apartment," he tells me a moment later, "it's all up in the attic room. You can select some shoes and then we need to go."

"You broke into my apartment?"

"I had a key," he smirks.

"You are an absolute psycho" I seethe.

"Off you go, little bird, times ticking."

Just like he said, all my clothes and shoes have been bought here, they have been unpacked and folded away, my shoes lined up in the closet, my toiletries in the small bathroom. Well at least he's not expecting me to share his room. Waking up with him was terrifying to say the least, especially since I had curled up like a fucking cat right up against him. His arm was around me, holding me close. I got the fuck out of that situation quickly. It didn't even occur to me at the time I could have probably offed him in his sleep, my only thought was not waking him and having to face whatever the fuck that was.

I choose a pair of small heels and sit on the bed to strap them on. I had no idea what Alexander was planning but I already knew I wouldn't like it.

I meet him in the foyer, swallowing down the anxiety.

He looks casually my way, hands buried in his pockets. He nods to a guy behind me and takes my arm, guiding me out the front door. I suck in a breath of fresh air, turning my face to the slight breeze as it teases my curls. I'm ushered into the back of black SUV but it doesn't go unnoticed the number of guys that follow us out, piling into 4 more SUVs identical to this one. Alexander slides in next to me, looking down at his phone. The driver doesn't say a single thing to either of us, but he doesn't look like a normal chauffeur. Which probably means he's one of the copious employees Alexander has. He looks hard, unforgiving, and ruthless.

Perfect.

With a huff I slide down into my chair and stare out the window as we set off.

"Let's cover some rules for this evening, shall we?" Alexander drags my attention away from the moving scenery.

I roll my eyes which earns me a scolding look.

"Firstly, you try to run and I've given instruction to shoot first, ask questions later," he tells me seriously, "unless you want a bullet hole in that tight little body of yours, I suggest you don't leave my side. Secondly, you do everything I tell you to."

"You're a control freak, you know that?"

"Do you understand?"

"Yes sir," I grumble with another eye roll.

We're in the car for about twenty minutes but I recognize where we are the moment we pull up outside the club. His club. My door is opened and Gruff holds out a hand to help me out the vehicle.

"Well hi, Gruff," I give him my fakest smile, "such a gentleman."

"Gruff?" His brows draw down.

"Yeah, you know, because you're so grumbly and growly."

"What?"

"Never mind," I pat his cheek condescendingly which earns me a growl that makes me laugh, proving my point.

Alexander is shooting daggers at me, teeth clamped tight.

"Well come on then," I snap, "or are we here just to have a mothers meeting in the street?"

A couple of his men eye me, confusion pulling down their brows, "Such a smart mouth," Alexander tuts.

I'm guided into the club with Alexander on one side and Gruff on the other, Lex's hand is on the small of my back and I'm sure anyone looking in from the outside would see this as intimate. We don't enter through the main entrance though, instead through a side door that drops immediately to a set of stairs I almost tumble down. A hand wraps around my arm to stop the fall but not a word is spoken. Gruff goes first, followed by me and then Alexander behind. I feel his presence like a shadow following me, the heat from his body consumes me, making it hard to breathe.

We enter through another door and what I'm seeing is nothing like upstairs. This is a completely different club, dirty, erotic, down right illegal. People snort white powder up their noses whilst others grope the women riding their laps, dressed in nothing but a pair of panties. Low music plays through unseen speakers and the scent of cigar smoke and whiskey permeates the air. There are security guards posted every few feet, watching the crowd. There are some very familiar faces here, the police chief, the port authority chief, even the fucking mayor.

Jesus Christ.

Whilst their wives and children are at home these guys are playing with the underground criminals and it quickly dawns on me that Alexander doesn't just ooze power, he *is* the power. He runs this city not any of these guys. Not the mayor or the police, they answer to him, he's the one in control.

A girl dressed in a cute little baby-doll lingerie set sashays towards us though her eyes are for Alexander only. When she finally reaches us, her manicured nails tickle down the front of Alexander's shirt, fingers tucking into the holes between the buttons.

Jealousy stabs me hot and deadly, and I have to stifle the need to yank her hair. I'm not able to stop the growl though which has Alexander peering down at me with amusement.

"Lex," her voice is low and sultry whilst she eye fucks him shamelessly. "Let me get you a drink."

Her brown eyes slip to me and one of her groomed brows quirks as she looks at me with disdain, her top lip curling.

My hands curl into fists, the nails biting into my skin.

"You can leave the newbie with Sasha, I'm sure she can train up the runt."

Alexander leans into her, and that jealously explodes. Fuck. I feel unhinged. I avert my eyes, I can't watch this shit and can't show him it affects me. Even though I try, I can't help but bring my eyes back. His hand is on the back of her neck and she rolls her head back, desire, like a flickering flame burns in her dark eyes. I'm sure she'd mount him right here and right now.

Just when I don't think he can surprise me anymore, his hand squeezes the back of her neck and he jerks her roughly towards him. There's no lust in his gaze as he looks at her, hatred, no that's too strong, but it isn't friendly, "Watch your mouth." He warns.

"W-what?" She stammers.

"You are replaceable," he tells her, "No one will miss

you, now, I think you owe Wren an apology."

Her eyes dart to me, "I didn't know she was with you." She pleads.

"Because you're not important enough to know anything." He releases her harshly and she stumbles in her heels.

"My apologies," she stutters before spinning and disappearing quickly, merging with the crowd to get away from Alexander.

Alexander drags me in close as we continue through the underground club until we hit an elevator. Inside it's just me, Gruff and him. The music from the club vibrates the steel walls but other than that and our breathing, the elevator is quiet. And tense. So very tense.

I practically sprint out when the doors open, putting distance between us. We are on a balcony, high above the dancers below. The music is loud, thumping through my body. I grip the handrail and peer down, if I could get down it would be so easy to slip into that crowd and disappear but I doubted Lex's threat to have me shot was empty.

I feel him step up behind me, caging me in with arms on either side of me, hands gripping the rail next to mine. His mouth comes down to my neck, where, so gently, almost as if he hadn't done it at all, he kisses the side of my neck.

My body stiffens with the heat that travels through my veins and I have to press my thighs together which earns me a deep vibrating chuckle. One hand releases the rail to hold my hip, fingers digging into my flesh, "You can fight it little bird, but eventually, you'll give in."

He's right. I've already proved, twice, that when it comes to him all my control slips right out the window. He does something to my body no man has ever been able to do.

He both terrifies me and intrigues me all at once. I should hate him, I should want to kill him, hurt him at least and yet I lean my back to his chest.

I know this man is a monster.

I know he's twisted. Cruel. Ruthless.

Everything about him should want me turning away from him and running as fast I can and yet, his darkness entices me. It draws me in, speaks to parts of me I didn't realize I had.

I don't want to want him, I really don't but sometimes we don't get what we want.

I'll fight, because that's my nature but eventually we all know I'll break and he'll have me.

And just like the little bird he thinks I am I'll be stuck in his cage with no hope of ever escaping.

19

Wren

I take it all back.

I want to kill him.

I stare at the glass in my hand and calculate the chances of being able to smash it and stab him with one of the shards.

"Come now, little bird, come sit your pretty little ass right over here," he taps his lap, daring me. I'm not sure if the challenge is to defy him or to do as he says.

"This chair is perfectly comfortable," I tell him, trying to sound sweet but missing the mark.

A couple of the guys around us grumble, unable to hide their amusement. Lex throws them a look that has them shutting up pretty quickly.

"It wasn't an option," he tells me, "do I need to come over there?"

My eyes dart around, so many people to be humiliated in front of and he already has so much power, I don't want to give him more. I bare my teeth at him as I stand, stomping my way to him ungracefully. When I reach him, I throw myself onto his lap hard, making sure to land my ass right on his cock and my elbow on his sternum. He grunts and sucks in a breath all at the same time. Good. I hope that hurt.

"Oh I'm sorry," I purr, sliding a hand down his front, "was that a little rough?"

His men can't contain it now, they burst out laughing. Lex ignores them as his eyes burn into me, seething.

"You keep fucking pushing little bird and I'm going to snap."

I shrug nonchalantly and down the rest of my vodka cranberry. Another is put in my hand immediately.

His words and his body are at war with each other. Anger and frustration radiate off him but the thick, hard cock pressing into my ass tells me he likes this. He likes it when I fight him.

I squirm on his lap and his jaw clamps tight as his hand comes down on my exposed thigh, fingers digging into my flesh. "Easy."

"Scared I'll make you blow in your pretty suit pants?" I taunt.

Push. Pull. Push. Pull. That was our relationship.

"You think I won't fuck you right here, right now?" He rasps, "I'll let them all watch. I'll let them all know who you belong too."

The thought both shocks and arouses me.

I flush, from my cheeks, all the way to my chest and further than that. I feel myself grow wet between the legs as my libido takes the reins here.

His eyes flash like molten silver in the darkness, "That gets you off, huh? Knowing all these people here will see me fuck you so hard you'll forget your own name." His hand gently caresses my thigh, fingers teasing at the hem but not slipping beneath the dress. "Does that make you wet, little bird? Do you want my cock in you?"

I open my mouth to retort but my words are stolen when he slams his mouth onto mine in a kiss so possessing it consumes everything. My thoughts, my words, they disappear as his mouth devours mine, his tongue dueling, teeth clashing. There's nothing gentle here. No sweetness, just pure primal need.

His hand finally skims up my thigh, following the slit and then he stills, both his hand and his mouth.

"Where are your panties?" He rasps under his breath.

I grin against his mouth, "This dress doesn't allow for underwear."

The grip on me turns hard, punishing but not painful, a warning.

"You'll never do that again."

"You don't control me."

With a single finger he finds my slit, swiping the digit

through my folds. The idea of this is wrong, so many people, so many eyes and yet the pleasure that makes my thighs tremble is a high I cannot resist. I feel my legs part to allow him in more and watch as his tongue traces his plump bottom lip.

His eyes narrow and he opens his mouth to speak but gets cut off.

"We have company," Gruff announces abruptly.

He snatches his hand away from my centre but continues to hold me, his eyes following the direction in which Gruff is looking, down towards the bar and dancefloor. Three men in suits stand menacingly but there's one who stands out. My father. Or who I thought was my father. Benjamin Lawson. He's staring right at me and there's nothing familial about it, he's furious, hatred pours off him as he stares at me. His eyes jump from me to Lex and back again.

"Who are they?" I hear Lex ask but I pay him no attention, my eyes stay trained on the man that raised me. Slowly, I see him reach into the inside pocket of his jacket.

"Lex!" I cry, grabbing him and pulling him to the ground just as a shot is fired. The glass panel of the balcony shatters into thousands of tiny pieces. Another shot has a man behind us hitting the deck hard. Our positions are suddenly reversed, with my body shielded by his.

Screams now overpower the music, the chaos and panic below palpable. Alexander's hands cup my head whilst his big body shields mine but he's shifting on top of me. We're out of sight of Benjamin but the shots keep coming.

A loud bang close to us makes my ears ring and then another, this one coming from directly above me. I twist my head, seeing Alexander holding out his gun.

The screaming continues but minutes pass and no more shots are fired.

"Get her out of here," Alexander growls as he climbs up off my body and then helps me to my feet. His eyes do a quick scan of my body, snagging on the cuts on my arms, hands and legs from the glass but I don't feel them. I don't feel anything other than sickness as I look down at the mass of panicked bodies, only seeing one.

Benjamin lays face down on the ground, a pool of blood blooming from his head. He's dead.

Greif robs my coherent thought. Despite it all, he was still the man that raised me, the man I called dad. We didn't have a great relationship, but we had something. And now he's dead. Killed by the man holding me as if I'm fragile.

"You killed him!" I scream.

"He tried to shoot you!"

Was he aiming for me? Why?

"Valentine wouldn't have sanctioned that," Gruff says, taking me when Lex hands me off. He tucks me into his side and I let him because if I don't, I'll end up a crumpled mess on the floor.

"No, that was rogue." Alexander looks back down, "Grab one of those guys he was with, we need answers.

174

Now."

Gruff says something to someone and I'm handed off
again. This one is unfamiliar and cold but he ushers me
to the elevator as he is told to do and walks close to me
as we make our way back through the underground area.
It doesn't appear they heard the commotion upstairs,
they all still sit and play and shove shit up their noses.
We're paid no attention and then we're stepping outside.
The cool air calms my heated skin. Screams and sirens
echo through the streets of Brookeshill. I'm guided into
a SUV and then we're peeling away from the sidewalk,
leaving the chaos behind.

Silence settles like a hammer, deafening. The shots fired
tonight continue to ring in my head and my stomach
rolls.

I have no idea what to think. Why would the man that
raised me try to kill me? Was it me or was it Lex he was
aiming for? Maybe it was both. I don't know.

I don't know anything anymore.

Lex

This is a fucking mess.

I may have control over this city but shit like this looks
bad. Cops have to get involved. Statements have to be

made. It has to look like all the processes are being followed. The club is empty now, the lights on revealing the complete mess of the place. There're shards of glass scattered across the floor, blood on the chairs, the walls.

It wasn't only Benjamin that took a bullet tonight. A girl, no older than twenty-two is sat at the edge of the club, looking pale and sweaty as the paramedics stabilize her ready for transportation to the hospital. She took a bullet to the arm. Another is dead right along with Benjamin Lawson. Both bodies are covered but their blood still stains my floor. One innocent and one not so much.

He had aimed for Wren, whilst she was sat in my lap, he had aimed for her and if she had not done what she did it's likely her body would be beneath one of those sheets.

Ryker speaks to an officer downstairs, weaving some story whilst I try to figure this shit out.

I had confirmation that we caught one of the guys that bolted after the first shots were fired, he's currently unconscious in the back of a car being transported to the compound. They'll string him up out in the barn ready for when Ryker and I get back.

This wasn't what I had hoped tonight would come to.

I knew Valentine's men would show, I knew they would report back that Wren is looking awfully cozy with the enemy and maybe it would have ended up with said girl naked and willing under me. But that shits not going to happen now.

Benjamin Lawson is dead. We have one guy and the

other guy is probably back in Valentine's ranks, reporting back.

But why shoot Wren? What was that angle?

Valentine wants his daughter back alive.

My mind whirls back to this so called Syndicate. I haven't managed to figure out anything about them but that'll change tonight. I had plans to interrogate one of Valentine's men and I have one ready and prime for the taking back at the compound.

As soon as this shit is sorted I'll be on my way. Appearances and all that shit require me to stay put for the time being but I'm itching to get back.

If only to make sure my little bird is okay.

20

Jex

"Get him conscious," I growl, wiping the blood from my hands on a rag I keep out here. Valentine's man sags in the chair, face a bloodied pulp but I'm far from done.

He's keeping his mouth closed for now but I can sense the crack coming, he'll break sooner rather than later.

"Where are you going?" Ryker asks, filling a bucket with cold water.

"To check on Wren."

Ryker laughs.

"What asshole?"

He shakes his head, "Nothing boss. You go check your girl."

I narrow my eyes but ultimately say nothing as I push out the doors of the barn and head the short distance to the house. My eyes travel upwards finding the light in the attic bedroom is on but the curtains are drawn. She could very well be asleep but a half hour ago I saw her peering out the window, staring at the barn. My men were keeping her in the house to stop her from getting too close to what we were doing but she had to know what was going on.

Inside, I wash my hands and then head up the stairs. Her bedroom door is ajar, golden light spilling out into the darkened hallway and a soft whimpering fills my ears.

She's crying.

Pausing, I listen for a moment. Hearing the deep shaky breaths she inhales and then blows out. A sniffle. Clearing her throat. Eventually I push in, finding her sat on her bed, legs drawn up to her chest. She's still in the dress she wore to the club and dried blood clings to her skin. She hasn't even cleaned herself up. Shards of glass are still embedded into her skin, they glint in the light above.

"You haven't sorted yourself out," I growl.

"Go away."

She turns her face away from me, hiding her tears.

With a grumble I head back out and down to the medical cabinet, fishing out my first aid kit before going back to her room. I don't have time for this shit but clearly she isn't going to do it herself and like fuck will I let another person touch her.

"I said go away!" She yells when I re-enter.

"I heard you," I snap back, crossing the room.

I grab her ankle and force her leg flat so I can get a better look at her knees. The glass is just on the surface, a few shards here and there and other than a few grazes it's nothing to worry about. Fishing out the tweezers, I start plucking out the small fragments and put them into a cotton pad. I do her other knee and then her hands and arms until her skin is clean and the wounds have been flushed.

I meet her eyes, red rimmed and slightly swollen. The tip of her nose is pink and her cheeks are flushed and she looks...broken.

"You killed him," her voice shakes.

"I did what I had to do." I affirm, "you need to shower and sleep."

"You're a monster."

"I never claimed to be anything else, little bird."

She scoffs and turns her face away, "I hate you."

"I know."

I did what was right. Benjamin Lawson would have killed her had he had the chance. If I had left him alive, I had no doubt he would have attempted it again. I just needed to figure out why.

You don't live with and raise a child without growing an attachment regardless of whether they are biological or not. Wren was looked after, cared for, given everything she could ever need by the same man who pointed a gun at her tonight.

"You killed him," she repeats, sniffing.

I understood. I did. Regardless of the situation he was the only man she called father and I took that away, leaving her with nothing. The familial bond overshadows his betrayal. The fact that he failed means she's looking through rose-tinted glasses, unable to fully comprehend what he attempted tonight.

"He would have killed you."

"Then maybe you should have let him."

"I'm not going to let anything happen to you."

"It's funny," she snaps, "I was fine before *you* showed up. My life was normal. Now? Now it's a fucked up mess and I'm suddenly living in a nightmare where my own father wants me dead and the man I'm currently *fucking* wanted me dead only a few days ago."

She's too wired right now, too emotional and I currently don't have the patience to deal with it.

"Shower. Bed." I order.

"Asshole."

"Don't push me, Wren."

She climbs off the bed, wincing a little as the skin on her legs stretches and moves, disturbing the grazes. She comes to stand in front of me, tilting her chin so she's looking down her nose at me.

"I saved *your* life," she jabs her finger into the centre of my chest, "Even if he were aiming at me, that bullet would have hit you too or maybe he would have shot me and then shot you immediately after. I fucking saved you, but I should have let you die. It would have made sense."

"You're right," I grab her wrist, hauling her to me. She lands hard against my chest, "You should have let me get shot but you didn't, and I now owe *you* a debt."

"What?"

"You saved my life, I owe you."

"Then let me go."

"I'm sorry," that's genuine, "I can't do that, even if I wanted to this war is on your doorstep now."

"Because of you."

I nod, confirming.

She sighs heavily and starts to push against my chest, trying to remove herself from me. There's no fight in her, no push, no heat. She just looks defeated and that's on me.

Guilt sits heavy in the centre of my chest.

I've been a part of this life for thirty one years, most of those have been spent with blood on my hands, lives have been torn apart because of me, both directly and indirectly and I've never felt an ounce of guilt. I've never cared enough to.

And yet this woman, *this fucking woman* has crawled under my skin.

I fucking care. And I hate it.

"Shower," I order. "Bed."

She laughs without humor, "Sure thing, *boss*."

I watch her saunter out of the room and towards the bathroom here on the top floor, hypnotized by the sway of her hips and then she slams the door. I wait until I hear the water turn on and then wait a little bit longer for the door to open and close and then I leave.

Back in the barn, Ryker has the guy awake. He's crying. Fucking pussy.

I grab a chair and slam it down in front of him, the sudden thud making the guy jump.

"What's your name?" I ask as I take a seat in front of him, placing my ankle on my knee and hooking my fingers behind my head casually.

This I can do. This I don't feel guilt for.

The man looks at me with glassy blood shot eyes, "Harry."

"Okay, Harry, we can get this over with really fucking quick, just tell me what you know."

"Fuck you Silver scum."

I laugh. "Wrong answer."

I hold my hand out to Ryker who places several paperclips in my palm. I begin to unbend them, straightening out the small rods of metal.

"What are you doing?" Harry stammers with wide eyes.

"Hand."

"No!" Harry panics as Ryker grabs his tied hands and drags them forward, forcing the fingers out flat on one hand. "No!"

"Are you going to talk?"

He doesn't answer.

I place one of the rods underneath the middle fingernail, pushing just a little, "Last chance."

"Fuck you!" Harry growls.

I jerk forward, embedding the paperclip so far down beneath the fingernail I'm sure it's touching his knuckle bone. Harry howls and I move to the next finger, doing the same thing on that one. Blood and tears mix together. I move to the next finger.

"Wait!" Harry cries, the third paperclip is already in position. I twist it a little, forcing it further down slowly, "wait!"

"Talk."

"You don't understand," he pleads, "They'll kill me."

"You're a dead man anyway, Harry, how you go, however, is entirely up to you."

He frowns.

I sigh, "You see, I'm just going to keep hurting you Harry, the longer your mouth stays silent the longer it will go on. I'll keep you alive but it's going to be painful. Want to know what I'm going to do next?"

His eyes are wide, begging for mercy. I have no mercy

for him.

"Next, I'm going to use this little thing right here," I pick up the peeler from the floor. It's rusted and dirty but the blade on it is sharp, "And I'm going to peel off your skin, starting at your feet until I get to your face. If you talk, tell me what I need to know, I'll make it quick."

"I have a wife," he begs.

"And she's going to be a widow regardless. Your choice Harry."

"Okay," he sobs, "okay."

"There's a good chap." I nod, pulling out the paperclip still waiting to be embedded into his finger and throw it to the floor. "Now, why the fuck did Benjamin Lawson try to shoot Wren tonight?"

He swallows, "That bitch is a traitor."

My fist is quick to connect to his jaw, "Don't make me hurt you more, Harry."

He spits blood onto the floor and glares at me, "she's a Valentine and she's fraternizing with you. It makes her a traitor."

"How can the girl be a traitor when up until a few days ago she had no idea Marcus Valentine even existed."

"It doesn't matter. The moment she found out she should have put a bullet in your head."

"Well she didn't so I guess I win that one. Now answer the question, Benjamin Lawson raised that girl and now he wants her dead, why did Valentine order the hit?" I know he didn't but I have to ask anyway, cover all my ground.

"Valentine is a fucking useless piece of shit," Harry spits again, "ever since you took his girl he's been distracted. Edgy. Damn right nasty and is not meeting his end of the bargain."

"What bargain?"

Harry groans, "Valentine is working with another organization, one that has the power to take you out."

I laugh, "Sure they do, if they had the power why aren't they here themselves."

"How do you know they're not?"

"So this organization, what are the called?"

"The Syndicate."

"And so the Syndicate contacted Valentine and told him to start a war with a family that has more connections than he'll ever have. Why?"

"They promised him the city if he did it. But then you went and fucked it up!"

"By taking his daughter." I nod.

"Yes."

"Okay, so that doesn't explain the hit on Wren."

Harry winces as he fidgets in the chair but he doesn't actively speak. With the paperclips still in my hand, I grab one and jab it under his fingernail so hard and so fast it embeds all the way in, leaving just a glint of metal hanging out the top.

Harry screams.

"Talk!"

"Okay, okay!" Harry sobs, "We were tipped off that you had the girl at the club and the syndicate contacted Lawson, told him if he got rid of the distraction he'd be rewarded. If he got you too, they would have killed Marcus and put him in charge."

I sigh. Power like that will definitely turn a man like Lawson.

I glance at Ryker who's watching this whole thing with narrowed eyes and a locked jaw, "This Syndicate," I continue, "Why my city?"

Harry laughs then, manically, "Not just your city asshole. All of them. They're the biggest underground organization the world has ever seen and once they have you, because they will have you, they'll take down the rest."

I stand from the chair and pull out my gun, lining it up with Harry's head. I promised it would be quick and I'm a man of my word.

My finger squeezes the trigger without a second thought. The loud bang ricochets off the walls of the barn, the bullet slicing through muscle and bone.

But despite gleaming the information from him I don't feel any better.

In fact, I feel like shit has yet to really hit the fan but

when it does, because it will, I will be ready.

I have to be.

21

Wren

The gun shot startles me where I lay in bed. My room is dark, my hair still wet from the shower and soaking the pillow beneath my head, but I didn't have the energy or motivation to dry it.

I knew they were doing something dodgy out in that barn and that shot just confirmed it. He just killed a man. Two in one night.

How many others have there been? How many lives has this one man destroyed. Tens? Hundreds? Thousands?

I swallow down the fresh wave of nausea and roll away from the window.

Silence settles around the house again, so quiet I could hear a pin drop until the door downstairs opens and closes and his footsteps echo through the halls. How fucked up does it make me to hope he comes to my room? How depraved?

Am I as bad as him?

Could I kill a man in cold blood?

The thoughts swirl in my head, I'm lost in them until the creak of my door opening has my eyes shutting tight. I know it's him. No one else would have the nerve to barge into my room, not because they're afraid of me but because they're afraid of *him*.

"I know you're awake little bird."

I sigh and turn my back to him, facing the window again. The door clicks shut and for a moment I think he's left but then the soft pat of his feet echo in the darkness and the other side of the bed dips down as he settles his weight there. I don't have to wonder for long what he's doing as he pulls back the sheets and settles his body behind mine.

"What are you doing?" I whisper.

"This is what you do when someone needs comfort, is it not?"

"You want to show me comfort?"

"Shh, little bird." His arms wrap around me, pulling me close and tight. His chin rests gently on the crown of my head whilst his body molds to the shape of mine.

This is weird.

This man is a monster.

And yet I am finding exactly what he said. Comfort.

Safety.

It makes no sense to feel safe with the devil but that's exactly what settles over me and drags me into unconsciousness.

When I wake the following morning, my eyes feel like they're covered in sand and my head is clouded. His body is still a hard pillar behind me. We're in the same position as we fell asleep in and when I try to move out of his arms, they only band tighter around me.

"No, no," he grumbles sleepily, an air of boyish innocence lacing his tone, "just a while longer."

"We need to talk," I whisper.

"Jesus Christ woman," he growls, "it's not even seven."

"Would you prefer we spoke over morning coffee and breakfast in bed?" My voice drips with honey. Honey that's poisonous and will make your insides rot.

"Don't get fucking mouthy with me."

I swallow when I feel his thickness pressing against the base of my spine.

"I want to know what happened. All of it."

"I'm not at liberty of sharing those details with you."

"Then what are you are at liberty of sharing, hm? You killed a man last night. Actually two if you include Lawson."

Saying it out loud makes my throat feel scratchy.

"Yes."

"Who was the second?"

"His name was Harry."

"Do you feel guilty?"

Silence meets my question but then he sighs and answers, "No."

"You're evil."

"Evil has a lot of faces, little bird, what you and I classify as evil are very different."

"So what happens to him now?"

"He gets cleaned up."

"He disappears," I rectify.

"Yes."

"How long have you done this?"

"Always."

"And Lawson, it was me he wanted to hurt?"

"Yes."

"Are you sure?"

"If you need confirmation, Ryker was witness."

I scoff, "As if I'd believe he would tell me the truth."

"If I asked him to, he would."

"It's too early for this," I grumble.

"You wanted to talk," Alexander shifts behind me and then his body is gone. He sits at the edge, scrubbing his hands down his face.

"Well I apologize for wanting to understand how I fit into all of this."

"There's more going on than I realized but that's all you need to know." He stands and stretches, "You're safe here."

"With you." I deadpan.

His steel eyes trap me but he doesn't say anything, just stares, making me squirm in the bed. To break the stare, I climb out of bed and go to the bathroom, shutting and locking the door behind me. I lean against the wood, taking a deep breath.

When I come out twenty minutes later, my room is empty. The call for coffee is too strong to ignore and if this is how it's going to be I can't ignore it forever.

I dress in one of my favorite summer dresses seeing as the sun is blaring outside. I may not be allowed out the front door but I can sit in the window and pretend. Pulling my hair into a pony tail I rifle through the belongings he had delivered to the house, finding my pill packet.

I've missed so many, but I should be okay. I pop one out and swallow it down dry before stashing the packet inside my makeup bag and heading downstairs.

There's chatter in the kitchen, hushed voices and for a moment I think about hanging back and eavesdropping but the look I'm being thrown by one of Lex's guys has me reconsidering.

When I enter the large kitchen all talk stops. Three heads turn my way. Lex sits at the island, sipping at a coffee whilst Gruff AKA Ryker leans on the counter and the blonde who I now know is named Ainsley is perched on the counter, swinging her legs.

She cocks her head to the side, studying me before her eyes jump to Lex. His eyes peruse my body and one dark smudge of brow quirks in interest.

"Coffee," I grumble, stepping into the awkwardness. Ainsley moves out the way whilst I lean in to grab a cup and place it under the sprout on the coffee machine, but her eyes stay on me as if she can see right inside my head and pluck out all my thoughts.

"Ains," Lex's stern voice has her head snapping his way, "Can you do it or not?"

She scoffs, "Of course I can, I've already hacked his system once, getting back in will be piece of cake."

"Arrogance will get you killed," Gruff grumbles.

"Don't be a baby," she tuts, "I'm hardly facing down a firing squad behind a computer screen, plus I can hold my own." I feel her eyes back on me again. She's probably still pissed that I knocked her ass out that one time.

I'll do it again too.

When my coffee is done, I add a sugar and some milk and then saunter from the room again, leaving them to it. They won't discuss shit whilst I'm there that'll actually get me any valuable information, so what's the point in hanging around. I head towards a set of patio doors. There doesn't appear to be anyone around and I wonder how easy I could slip outside. Funnily enough my first thought isn't to run, I just want some air and some sun. I'm about to reach for the handle when the sound of gun being loaded has my head swiveling.

"Come away from the door, miss Wren," it's one of Lex's guys and the gun is pointed directly at me. He's not aiming for anything vital but it'll hurt nonetheless.

"I just want some air," I say to him.

"Orders are to not let you outside."

"Please" I beg, "I'll sit right there," I point to the set of chairs and table out on the patio, "You can even tie me down if you want. Just some air."

"I can't do that, Miss Wren."

"It's okay," Lex's voice startles us both, "Lower your gun."

"Sir?"

"Do it," Lex growls, "let her out."

The guy nods and holsters the weapon, frowning at me before slipping back into his position.

"Go ahead."

I pull the handle down and swallow, waiting for the shoe to drop.

"I can go?"

"On the patio, yes. But I think you know that if you run, I'll find you."

I knew it alright, and the thought exhilarated me. Maybe one day, I'll test the theory.

22

Lex

She curls up on the wicker chair, her summer dress falling lazily over her bent knees as she sips at the coffee in her hands. Her eyes are still slightly swollen though they look clearer than they did last night, not so clouded with emotion.

I couldn't expect her to understand, I couldn't expect her to be able to process what she saw like the rest of us would. She's been sheltered, kept in the dark and yet she's been a valuable player her whole life. It seems cruel to keep someone like her in the shadows.

If not me, it would have been someone else. Up until now no one paid much attention to Valentine, he was useless, not really a threat, more a nuisance until he decided to attack. Now I realize he's grown tired of being the little man in this world and is coming for the big guns. My city. Had he picked another city, another town, they would have picked apart his life too, found his weak spots and exploited them, who knows what could have happened to Wren then? There's so many ways girls like her could go missing and not every time means death.

This organization, the Syndicate, they are backing him and not knowing who they are or where they have come from puts me on edge. Being blind in a game like this has deadly consequences.

Leaving Wren on the balcony I head back through to the kitchen but bypass it instead and go to my study, pulling my phone from my pocket.

My father has been out of the game for months now, he left me fully in charge though I know he still has his fingers in the pot. There's no way in hell the old man would have just left. Even though his wife died and he was distraught, wrecked with grief, the city was his second love. Just like it was my grandfathers and his grandfathers. The Silver's own this city and have done for a long time, it's in our blood.

I dial my fathers number and settle down in the chair behind the desk, pulling up the camera feed, going to one in particular. It shows the back side of the house, positioned in a way that shows both the stretched lawn and the balcony where Wren sits. She's made me want *more.* An obsession I can't seem to shake, and I fear that if it is ever taken away, I'll never be the same.

She's as still as anything, the only giveaway that she's even real is the gentle way the wind teases her hair and her arms gently cradling the cup, bringing it to her lips every few minutes for a sip of her coffee.

The phone rings three times before he picks up.

"Son," he greets, his voice husky and rough from a lifetime of bad decisions.

"I need information."

"Well hello to you too."

"Hello," I grunt, "good enough?"

Me and my father didn't have a bad relationship, but it wasn't one filled with love and compassion either. No, I was raised on brutality and hostility. My mother was the one who showed me compassion. She was the one who nursed me and cradled me when I was a child, giving me at least some semblance of a normal childhood. I respect my father. I value him. But there was no compassion. The relationship between him and I seemed more like a business transaction, there was always an ulterior motive behind everything and even now, as I phone him and hear his voice on the other end of the line, I don't feel anything other than the need to find out more about this Syndicate. I didn't care to find out how he was doing, where he was or even if I'd ever see him again.

He chuckles, the laugh turning to a harsh cough, "What information?"

My eyes stay trained on the girl who's invaded my entire life. "The Syndicate. Who are they?"

"Where did you hear that name?"

"So you've heard of them?"

"Yes."

"What do you know?"

The line goes silent for a long time, long enough for me to pull the phone from my ear to check the call is still connected, "Not on the phone. I'm back in the city in soon. We'll meet to discuss it then."

"When? I don't have time for this," I growl. "Where the fuck even are you?"

"That's none of your business." He huffs, "Soon, Lex. See you then."

He hangs up. He doesn't offer anything more or anything less. My hands curl around the phone as frustration and anger war with each other inside me. I was blind. I was fucking blind and I had no way of knowing shit. I had to hope Ainsley with her technical skills could get me something but I was losing patience.

There was no way in hell I was letting this shit go or stay in limbo for a damn week let alone an infinite amount of time. I needed to find who this fucking Syndicate was and end them. Now.

My eyes stray to Wren once again. One of my housekeepers has stepped out onto the balcony with her and is passing her a coffee. She smiles and takes it. As the house keeper turns back, her face lifts to the camera.

I don't recognize her, and I know all my staff.

Fuck.

I bolt from the chair and sprint through the house, drawing my gun from the holster at my back, clicking off the safety. I spot her walking casually towards me, when she notices me there, she halts mid-step, eyes growing wide.

"Down!" I bellow.

My voice startles Wren behind her, still cradling that

cup of coffee. "Put it down, Wren." A sickness churns my gut, something akin to fear and panic.

She eyes me, the gun and then the coffee, her brows drawing together before she gingerly places the mug on the table and climbs from the chair.

"What's going on?" She asks.

"Down!" I yell again, directed to the intruder.

The commotion has drawn Ryker and Ainsley from the kitchen, the moment Ryker spots my weapon, he withdraws his own.

The woman before me lifts her hands slowly, bending her knees to lower herself to the floor.

"They made me," she cries.

I take a look at her, her skin is translucent, the bones on her face prominent as well as her collar bones and hands. She looks ill, malnourished. Her lips are cracked and her eyes are bloodshot.

"Face on the floor," I order, keeping my weapon trained on her with one hand, I beckon Wren to me with a curl of the finger on the other. The only reason I haven't shot her yet is because Wren is here. She's seen enough death in the last day, one more is not going to be added to the table.

Wren comes willingly though she is clearly confused. I tuck her into my side, turning my body to shield her.

"I didn't know she was your woman," the girl cries, "They didn't tell me that. They just said that she betrayed them, that she had to die and if I did it, they would let my sister go!"

"Do you know who I am!?" I growl.

She shakes her head.

I pass Wren off to Ryker who follows a similar move as me, tucking her to him and shielding her from whatever the fuck this is.

"What's in the coffee?"

"Cyanide."

Fuck.

They're not messing around. This Syndicate want Wren dead. A punishment to Valentine. I'd laugh if it wasn't so fucked up. Wasn't it me who had the same idea and now look at me, protecting the girl.

"Hands where I can see them," I tell her, "and then get up, slowly."

The girl raises her hands above her head and then slowly rises from the floor, keeping her arms above her head, "Ryker, take her to the barn."

"No!" Wren cries, "no don't do that."

"This isn't a time for mercy, little bird." I growl.

I hear the thud of someone's fist hitting flesh and I spin around, a blanket of fury making my blood boil so quick and fast I see red. Only what I expect to see and what I actually see are two very different things.

"She broke my fucking nose!" Ryker moans, cupping

his face. Wren's eyes widen as she rushes towards me, but she isn't looking at me. By the time I realize what the fuck is going on, Wren has ripped the gun from my hand and has pulled the trigger. The loud bang in the small hallway makes my ears ring.

 After the silence settles around us like a lead weight there are three thuds in executive order, one behind me and two in front.

23

Wren

I spin around, my fist colliding with Gruff's nose. It's the only way to get him to release me and he's not expecting it which is why it connects with as much power as I can muster. I cringe at the sound of my fist connecting with his flesh, the cartilage breaking under the pressure and then the outburst of blood that streams from his nostrils. I ignore the pain in my knuckles as I rip myself away from his body.

I can't let them hurt her. She was only here because someone else put her up to it. That's not fair. They didn't give her a choice.

I can see clearly she's unwell, malnourished, in need of a good bath and some food, probably medicine too. I thought the same when she bought me my coffee – *my poisoned coffee* – and I thought it strange then. All the staff Alexander has employed here look healthy, happy even and it begs the question if they really know what happens within these walls. She didn't look like she fit but then what did I really know about any of this? So I didn't question it. Not until Lex stormed towards us like a demon sent straight from hell, his weapon drawn and directed at the girl.

I rush towards Lex, I'll beg and I'll plead until he gives her mercy.

But all that changes when I lock eyes with the girl over Lex's shoulder. She's suddenly pulled her own gun and has aimed it for the back of Lex's head. Her hand shakes, her eyes wide with both vengeance and fear and the next thing I know, I'm ripping the gun from Lex's hand and pulling the trigger.

She goes down hard. Quick too, the bullet hole in her chest blooming red immediately. Her hands hold it, the blood seeping through her fingers as if to contain a leak. When her body finally hits the floor she's staring wide eyed at the wall.

Oh God.

Oh god!

I killed someone. Shit. I killed her for him!

The gun slips from my hand and hits the floor. Lex stares at me, seemingly frozen as the gun rattles against the hardwood floor and then my knees give out. The pain, the guilt, the nausea of what I've just done crippling me. My knees crunch on the hard surface as a sob rips from my throat.

What have I done!?

"S-she," I stammer, shaking my head, trying to form

words whilst my tongue refuses to cooperate, "she was going to kill you."

All I can see is the young girl in front of me, she can't be much older than me, her hair is blonde, ashy but greasy and dirty. Her eyes are a deep blue color and whilst her skin is pale and sickly, she has an olive complexion, one that probably glows had she been healthy.

"Clean it up!" Lex growls but I can't see him. I can't see the others either, just the dead girl. The one I killed. For him. For Lex.

Why did I do that? That's twice. *Twice*! Why the hell would I save a man who wanted me dead only a few days ago, save a man who is keeping me here against my will. He's a monster and yet I don't want him to leave. I need him.

I've never needed anyone but for some sick and twisted reason *I need him*.

How do you need a man you've only known for a few weeks? How has he suddenly become so important to me that all his misdeeds don't even account for anything?

His body steps in front of mine, blocking off the image in front of me. With her out of sight the world comes back to me. I see Ryker step around me, Ainsley too but they keep a wide berth, making sure not to touch me. There's shuffling, the movement of something heavy being dragged across the floor but I can't see. Tears stream from my eyes, wetting my cheeks. I didn't think I had any left to give but I can't seem to stop them. I sob and I cry until Lex leans down and gently lifts me from the floor.

My legs feel like jelly, weak, like the bones have turned to mush but it's not painful. They just don't work. My stomach rolls.

When walking doesn't seem to work, Lex leans down and swoops my legs from underneath me, hoisting me into the cradle of his arms. My arms automatically loop around his neck.

"Don't look," he whispers, "Tuck your face to my chest. Don't look."

So much death. So much blood.

I cry into his chest, wetting his white shirt as he carries me through the house and towards his bedroom.

He gently places me on the bed where I immediately curl into a ball.

He must have gone into the bathroom at some point because now I hear running water but I didn't realize he had left until he's in front of me again.

"Come, little bird, sit up."

I do.

He slides my dress from my body, throwing it behind him and then removes my underwear. It doesn't feel sexual, but my body responds to his touch, nonetheless.

I'm sick.

Who gets aroused at a time like this? After they just killed someone.

I don't have time to think about that for long because the next minute he's lifting me from the bed and guiding me to the bathroom. The tub is almost full but the faucet is still running as he guides me towards it, coaxing me into the hot water. Steam rises from the surface and I sink down, letting the water run over my skin.

"Shh," Lex soothes, "It's okay."

"I hurt her," I whisper.

"It's okay."

I shake my head. How could it be okay?

"You're in shock. Wren, take a minute, breathe."

"Get in with me?" I ask, my voice quiet.

"You want me in there?"

I nod. "Please."

"Okay, give me a minute." He turns to leave but my arm dashes out, my wet fingers hooking against his shirt.

"No don't leave."

He puts his hand over mine and gently pries my fingers off. With his silver eyes holding mine he strips from his suit, revealing all his hard, lethal muscle and for a minute I forget. I revel in the brutal beauty of this man. I commit each scar to memory, each roll and flex of his muscles, the smattering of hair at his navel that travels all the way down to the pubic hair around his groin.

He moves with all the lethal grace of a lion stalking a gazelle. When he climbs into the tub and lowers himself

208

behind me, the water level rises quick, spilling over the rim of the tub but he doesn't seem to care as his arms reach around and drag me to his chest, settling me into the cradle of his thighs as his arms gently stroke down my arms.

I never thought this man could do gentle.

"You make it look so easy," I say quietly. "how?"

"It wasn't always. But I turn it off, little bird, I don't feel."

"I killed someone."

"It's okay."

"It's not okay."

"Shh, little bird, relax."

Lex

This should never have happened. I'm distracted. That's twice now, in less than twenty four hours, that I have been distracted and people have gotten hurt.

I don't care much for the girl, despite her pleas, I wouldn't have shown mercy. There will be no mercy for anyone who comes for Wren.

Like this city, she belongs to me.

When Wren is finally asleep, her head in my lap whilst I gently stroke her hair, wild and unruly, I climb from the bed, turning out the light.

The shock will be with her for some time but she's strong and eventually she'll realize she did the girl a kindness. I wouldn't have made it that quick.

"How did she get in?" I ask when I hit the kitchen. Both Ainsley and Ryker are still here, Ryker now sporting a swollen nose with dark bruising starting to appear beneath his eyes.

"Here," Ainsley points to a camera feed from seven thirty this morning. Most of my house keepers stay on sight in the small annexes set down near the gates but some travel in. They are vetted and searched at the gates before being allowed entry.

I watch the feed and as the guard stops a vehicle I see her slip in whilst he's distracted. She darts left and tucks herself into a hedge line against the wall. It's another hour before she reappears again, further up the gardens, close to where Wren is on the balcony. I didn't notice her when I was watching the feed because she's not in direct line of the camera but is on the one looking from another direction. She seems to pause when she sees her on the balcony.

The girl was smart. She knew if she shot her there and then there was no way she would be getting off this land, so she slipped in through a back entrance. After that you can guess how she maneuvered through the house, posing as a housekeeper. No one would have questioned her, I have several members of staff here everyday, and she looks innocent and plain enough to fit right in. She probably avoided the kitchen Ryker and Ainsley were in, they would have noticed she didn't quite fit because they'd never seen her before, and they always know who I employ, so she would have gone to one of the other three kitchens in this place to concoct that little coffee she presented Wren with.

I'm too distracted. If it weren't for my current obsession with the girl sleeping in my bed upstairs none of this would be happening. I don't make mistakes, but I've made several now and each time they put her in danger.

I needed to end this.

Marcus Valentine needed to go followed by this Syndicate.

No one threatens what is mine.

No one makes an attempt on something that belongs to me.

I'm the motherfucking king and it's time I remind them of that fact.

24

Lex

This was war. There's been more blood on these streets these past few days than there has been for years.

We Silver's had instilled enough fear into those who questioned us that there was no need for the violence. People fell in line wherever we went but now, now that was slipping.

Valentine's men line up in front of me, on their knees facing the water at the docks. In the distance a fog horn sounds, cutting through the mist that rolls across the dark waters. Around me containers are stacked high, cranes and forklifts abandoned.

I twist the silencer onto my Glock, my hands encased in leather gloves.

A whimper and a sniffle echo through the abandoned shipping yard.

Fucking weak.

And they think they can take over my city.

This shit is laughable.

"Eeny, meeny, miny, moe," Ryker taps the barrel of his gun to each of their heads as he sings the nursery rhyme, he repeats it a few times before stopping at the middle guy. There's five lined up in total. When the barrel rests on the base of his skull, the guy outright cries. His sobs ricochet around the yard, bouncing off the still waters of the docks. Ryker doesn't hesitate, he pulls the trigger, the bullet ripping through his skull like it's no more than butter. He hits the concrete hard, blood pooling from his face.

"So who's next, should we sing again?" Ryker taunts.

I've grown tired though. I pull the trigger four times, ending them. Five more deaths. Five more bodies. I'll take them all out one by one if I must.

"Dump them on the south side, make sure it's Valentine or his men that find them."

Ryker nods as I climb back into my SUV and head across the city, back towards the compound.

The radio is pulling the current news bulletin.

"Club Silver has reopened its doors after a gunman opened fire on the crowd. Two dead, one was student Robbie Hill and the other was the shooter himself. At this time, there is no known association to Club Silver or the owner Alexander Silver, but investigations are still ongoing."

I hit the button to silence it and instead listen to the tires of my car on the road. It's quiet, the streets empty bar a few other cars. It's too late for many people to be out but

I could guarantee the city centre, namely the areas around my club would be packed. I avoid it on purpose, taking a few back roads to hit the highway that would lead me to the compound.

My bright white lights cut through the darkness until I eventually see the lights of the mansion like a beacon, drawing me in though I know it isn't the house making me put my foot down and speed up. It isn't my bed or the comfort of the four walls, it's her.

Wren fucking Valentine.

I'm well and truly fucked.

At the gates, I lean out and press my finger to the scanner, waiting for the green light and the beep to sound and then the gates begin to slide open. Since the incident with the house keeper there are constant guys patrolling the grounds. Call me paranoid but until this shit is over, I won't be making anymore mistakes or taking any chances.

I roll the car to a stop and throw the keys to one of my guys for him to put it in the garage and then take the steps two at a time, pushing the wide doors open. I scan all the rooms on the lower floor looking for her, but she isn't down here and as I climb the stairs the sound of soft cries and moans fill my ears.

I pick up the pace, heading up to the attic room where the sounds are coming from, throwing the door open.

Wren writhes in the bed, the sheets tangled around her limbs as she thrashes in her sleep. The cries are coming from her but she's alone in here. Alone with the demons plaguing her dreams.

She's been like this a few times since the house keeper and I don't know how else to help her. She hates me, or so she says but I know the truth.

It's me who brings her comfort, it's me who settles her dreams and allows her to sleep easy. She can scream and fight me for now, but the truth will eventually come out.

I cross the room and like every night, I scoop her up, pushing the covers from her body. She's damp from sweat, her skin sticky and like every night I take her down to my room, her grumbling and pouting like a child and shove her into the shower to wash away the dreams.

And like every night, she slips her head into one of my t-shirts that falls to mid-thigh on her tiny frame and climbs under the blankets, curling her body into mine.

Yeah, she hates me alright.

"You still fighting me baby?" I drawl into the darkness.

"I'll always fight you." She mumbles, pressing her mouth to my bare chest.

The touch of her lips to my skin sends a spike of pleasure down my spine.

"Careful little bird," I warn.

Her fingers curl into my stomach, her nails biting against my skin enough to make me hiss through my teeth as she pushes her hips forward, grinding herself against my leg.

I growl as I grip the hem of my t-shirt covering her body and rip it straight off, leaving her bare to me. With the curtains open I see her bathed in the silver glow of the moon, it caresses her pale skin, making her seem ethereal, like she has a halo of light around her. So fucking beautiful, all toned muscle and smooth curves.

She groans when I force her to her knees, bending her forward so her ass is in the air.

"You want this," I rasp.

Her answer is to back up, pressing her ass to my hard cock, straining to be free from my boxer shorts.

"My little bird," I coo.

"You're the devil," her voice comes out on a breath, barely audible above my own rough breathing.

My hand smooths down the curve of her spine, feeling each bump of her vertebrae until I find her waist, my hands cupping her sides. She's so tiny, so fragile. I could break her so very easily.

She moans as I press my erection against her centre, the warmth of her seeping through the thin material. Pulling back, I slide the boxers off and reposition behind her, pressing the crown of my cock to her entrance, warm and wet, ready for me.

"That's where you're wrong little bird," I tease her, pushing only an inch into her tight pussy, "the devil was once an angel and I've never been good. I'm the monster under your bed," another inch forward, "I'm the thing that goes bump in the night and stalks you in the shadows." Another inch and I begin to feel my restraint slipping as her warm core envelopes and tightens around my shaft. "I'm your motherfucking nightmare."

I slam forward, impaling her on my cock so hard she screams and her fists ball the sheets, nails scratching against the cotton.

I withdraw and slam forward again.

"Say it!" I demand on a growl.

"Fuck you." She cries.

Always pushing me. Always testing me.

"Say it!" I bellow, pounding into her hard. My fingers bruise her hips as my relentless thrusts jolt her body against the mattress, "Tell me little bird, tell me who you fucking belong to."

She moans loud, her cries of ecstasy causing my spine to stiffen, my balls to draw up tight, "Say it and I'll reward you baby."

She cries out when I withdraw, halting her impending orgasm. I tease forward, the walls of her pussy trying to clamp down and take purchase on my cock, "Say it."

I tease that sweet spot inside her with the crown of my cock, feeling her spasm, wanting – no – *needing* more.

"You!" She snaps, "I belong to you!"

"Good girl," I reach around and pinch her clit between my fingers whilst slamming into her hard enough to make her bones rattle. Her scream pierces the darkness of the bedroom.

Her orgasm is quick and violent, it clamps around my cock like a vice, holding me in place, drawing my own climax from my body with force.

I roar my release, my fingers biting into her flesh whilst she continues to spasm around me.

Spent and exhausted, I collapse down next to her, drawing her body into mine.

I liked having her this close, I liked her warmth on my skin, her breathing syncing with mine.

"I hate you," she whispers.

I smooth down her wild, still slightly damp hair, inhaling her sweet scent like it's a drug and I'm the addict.

She doesn't hate me. Not at all and the feeling is mutual.

The feeling is dangerous. It's what's likely to get me killed at the end of this but I've never been good with warnings.

I'm the king and this is my kingdom and all kingdoms need a queen.

25

Wren

I hate you.

I hate you.

Those words leave my mouth far too often and yet every time I use them, I find I don't mean them quite as much as the last. No, hate isn't something I feel towards this man any more and that simply terrifies me.

He terrifies me.

He's a man that commands a room, commands respect, whether that be through fear or loyalty, he's lethal, brutal, vengeful and I'm drawn to that. His presence makes people cower, when he walks into a room he doesn't have to say a word for everyone to *know* the man is king.

His darkness calls to me. His violence and menace entices me.

I know how stories like ours end but I'm still the little idiot moth drawn to the flame, I find myself falling into him, waiting for the burn. There isn't much I can do to stop it, I'll just revel in the pain as the flames devour me.

His possessiveness, the way he handles me, both acting as if I'm fragile and the strongest woman he's ever known, I can't help but let my stupid heart fall for him. There's something so very satisfying about knowing he's a monster that is only soft with me.

His thick arms are banded around me, holding me to his chest, his heat enveloping my body like a caress. His breathing is soft and gentle, brushing the fine hairs at the nape of my neck as he breathes deeply in his sleep. It's still dark out, I can see the moon hanging fat and swollen in the night sky, silver light bathing the compound grounds.

I've seen more people this week than I ever have since being here, armed guards, men employed by Lex standing in the halls. They pay me no mind bar the odd hello but Gruff still isn't speaking to me after I broke his nose.

I apologized. He wasn't having it.

Gently, I roll onto my back and then turn again until I'm facing the man of my nightmares.

His beauty is cruel and unforgiving, merciless, all hard lines and sharp edges. My fingers tickle over the thick hair growing around his mouth and up his cheeks and then further up into his thick mane of hair, the strands soft between my fingers.

Slowly, I lean forward, allowing myself a kiss against

his pillowy lips. When I pull away his eyes are open, staring at me, the silver irises so bright they rival the moon.

He reaches up and untangles my hand from his hair, pulling it down until my fingers hover in front of his mouth and gently, so very gently, his presses a kiss to every finger.

My heart stutters in my chest at the intimate way his lips press against my skin, the air from his breath caressing my skin almost as softly as his lips.

The room is silent other than the inhales and exhales of our breathing but in the quiet I swear a thousand words are said. Words neither of us would ever dare to vocalize. When he releases my hand, he brings his own to my face, feathering the tips down the side of my face, down the curve of my neck and over my shoulder. I'm still naked from our earlier adventures and I know he is. I press the palm of my hand against his sternum, feeling the muscles coil and jump under my touch. I love how he reacts to me, even from the first moment we met, there was no way he could hide his reaction to me, I felt it in the way the air around us charged with tension and electricity, in the way we both exploded like storms whenever we touched.

"Little bird," he mumbles, the first one to break this mutual silence.

"Twisted king," I reply.

His deep chuckle vibrates through me, "What am I going to do with you?"

I push his shoulders, forcing him onto his back and then

straddle his narrow hips. My eyes devour his naked torso, his hard muscles, the definition around his pecs and the V that carves his hips. I feel him grow hard between my legs, his cock pressing into my sensitive flesh. His hands squeeze the tops of my thighs as his eyes narrow in on me. Rolling my hips I rub against his shaft, pleasure shooting up my spine.

"I want you," I admit.

"I thought you hated me," he smirks, his fingers biting into the fleshy areas of my legs. When I grind my hips again his eyes roll back and his fingers tighten, his control becoming paper thin.

"Shut up," I growl.

That deep chuckle shoots straight to my clit and in one quick movement, he shifts my weight and pistons his hips, entering me in one swift move. I cry out into the darkness, feeling him stretching and filling me in the most painfully pleasurable way.

"Fucking ride me, baby," he growls, "let me watch you."

His filthy mouth fuels my need to own him, have him in everyway and with him buried so deep I begin to roll my hips, using his chest to help steady me. His breathing is heavy, and his moans fill the darkness. He takes his hand away from my thigh and runs it up the centre of my chest, through the valley of my breasts until his fingers curl around my throat. His hand tightens, fingers pressing in at the edges of my windpipe and he jerks me forward.

My mouth slams against his violently, his teeth pulling

at my bottom lip, nipping hard enough to draw blood that dribbles onto my tongue.

"That's it," he rasps into my mouth, that hand still banded around my throat and now one in my hair, tugging my head back so my neck is stretched out and open for him. In this position I have no control, I have no way to move and he knows it. On my knees, straddled over his hips he pounds into me from below, holding my head back, the sting on my scalp and the pressure on my throat only adding to the pleasure wracking my system.

"You're such a good girl," he growls against my throat, "so good."

I can't talk, I can only scream for him, I can only let myself fall harder and harder with each deep thrust and whispered praise.

I wake to an empty bed and serious cramps. Guess I don't have to worry about the pill not working anymore. On a groan, I roll from the sheets and trudge across the quiet bedroom, slipping into the shower immediately. The hot water soothes the ache in my back but does nothing to stop the cramping in my stomach. I wash away the night, the scent of Lex on my skin and between my thighs before wrapping myself in a towel and heading up to the attic bedroom where I know I saw some of my toiletries in the bathroom.

I sort myself out and dress in baggy sweats and a sweater before tying my hair into a bun that sits atop my head messily. I need to go to the supermarket and pick up more things but I highly doubt Lex is going to let me go.

I no longer feel like a prisoner here, but I don't feel free either.

My feet shuffle back down the stairs and towards the kitchen where I hear the coffee maker whirring and spitting out coffee. It isn't Lex I find there though but Gruff.

"Gruff!" I beam at him.

He looks at me over his shoulder and heaves a sigh. The bruising on his face has gone down a lot since I hit him but he isn't over it clearly.

"Are we still sour about the whole nose thing?"

"You broke my nose," he grumbles.

I shrug, "I guess we're even."

"How are we even?" He exclaims.

"You kidnapped me."

He opens his mouth to say something but then promptly shuts it, his teeth rattling together.

"Where's Lex?" I ask, accepting the coffee from him.

"Busy, he left me watching you."

"I don't need a babysitter."

Gruff scoffs, "Trouble follows you Wren, of course you need a babysitter."

My brows pull low, I have no idea how all of this shit has been turned on me. I wouldn't even be a part of this mess if it wasn't for this asshole in front of me and the one currently off galivanting doing god knows what.

I try not to think about it too much.

This has all been a game for them, one that has gotten out of hand. I wanted no part in it though we don't always get what we want.

My stomach cramps painfully. I'd always suffered with bad menstrual cramps for the first day or so of my cycle but it seems this one is really knocking me for six.

Gruff frowns, stepping towards me, "What's wrong?"

"Aw, look at the big scary man showing concern," I grit my teeth.

"Seriously, Wren, what is it?"

I wave a hand, "Don't worry. It's just mother nature taking her course."

Gruff visibly winces, taking a step back which earns a laugh from me. He has to be fucking with me. He's got to be.

"Can I, uh, can I do anything?"

I spin on the stool, facing away from him, my eyes suddenly colliding with the hall where I shot the intruder. Bile rises in my throat and I force myself back around.

I killed someone. My nightmares remind me of that fact every day, her face haunts my dreams, the sound of her body hitting the floor plays on repeat inside my ears.

"Wren?" Gruff presses.

"Yeah, actually, I need to go to the store."

"That'll be a no."

I narrow my eyes at him, forcing my mind away from the images trying to capture my attention, "What do you mean no?"

"You can't leave here."

My teeth grit so hard together the enamel feels like its chipping, "I need the store. I want to get some things. I can't stay inside this house forever, Gruff."

"Stop calling me Gruff," he huffs.

"Fine, *Ryker*, I need to go to the store. Take me."

He laughs, "No chance."

"Ryker!" I seethe. "Nothing will happen. Just take me to store, I'll even let you escort me round and you can bring me right back."

He's shaking his head before I've even finished my sentence, "So you can run?"

"I'm not going to run," it was the truth. Not because I wouldn't be able to, if we were out in public there would be undoubtedly every opportunity to make a break for it, but I find the need or want to run is gone. Again, terrifying, but I'm learning to take things as they come.

These *feelings* for Lex stop those urges, they stop the need to get away and replace it with the desire to get closer, despite the blood staining his hands.

He scoffs again and the sound grates on my every nerve, "I swear to God." I don't finish the threat.

"What do you need? I'll go and leave one of the guys here to watch you."

I cock a brow, my lips curling with satisfaction. I've only ever seen men around here and whilst there are a few out there who would buy the shit I need, these guys aren't it. Their fragile masculinity couldn't take the hit.

"Well, I need sanitary products Gruff, you know, tampons, towels. Maybe some heat pads and lots of icecream. Oh and chocolate. Maybe some popcorn?"

His face is a mask of horror, "On second thoughts, I'll send Ainsley."

He pulls out his phone and dials but after the fifth attempt, he huffs in annoyance, taps at his phone and puts it to his ear again but again, whoever he dials must not pick up because he throws the device down on to the counter and stares at me angrily like I'm the one dodging his calls.

"So are we going?"

"No, you'll have to wait."

I sigh dramatically and I really shouldn't, *really* I shouldn't but clearly I'm not above a little manipulation. "Well, fine, then, if you're happy for me to be in pain all day *and* bleed through then," I shrug, like it's not a big deal. I mean none of that shit will happen, I'm covered for at least today, "but I guess you'll have to explain that to Lex."

"Fuck." He growls. "Fuck."

"So, your choice, Gruff."

"Get your shit, you have ten minutes to get your shit and then we're out of there."

26

Wren

"I don't like this," Gruff says for the hundredth time since we pulled up outside the small supermarket and parked the giant SUV.

"I mean, we could have taken a less conspicuous car, you know?" I shrug like that's the problem.

Truth be told, I hadn't really thought this plan through, I just needed to get out the house and I did need the store. I didn't think about how nervous I'd be when I got there. After all, it's twice someone has tried to kill me, first my father, who's not actually my father and then a seemingly harmless housekeeper.

But realistically, how is anyone going to know I'm here?

Paranoia has no place inside my head so I tilt my chin up and pop the door. It's warm today making the sweats and sweater a bad move but I needed comfy rather than convenient.

"Hey, wait!" Gruff scrambles to get out the car and then he's right next to me, curling his hand around my arm, not hard or aggressively, more protective than anything else.

"It's okay," I tell him, patting the paw that circles my bicep, "let's just get what we need and go home."

He grunts and we make our way across the lot. I glance sideways at him, he looks out of place next to me, dressed in his pristine tailored suit, Italian loafers loud on the asphalt as his steps cover more ground than my little ones could ever hope to achieve. We look every bit the fucked up pair that we are. The air conditioning of the store hits me like a bucket of water, refreshing considering the heat outside and we move quickly to one of the aisles containing fresh produce.

"Doing some grocery shopping at the same time?" I ask.

Gruff drags me through the aisle, turning at the end until we find the one we are looking for. His nerves are rattling my own.

I realize there would be no real way of defending ourselves here, so open and public, it's not like Gruff could whip out his gun and shoot someone should he need to. No that shit is done behind closed doors with no witnesses.

They may run the city but there are still rules.

I stop at the section where the products are and pluck the bits and pieces that I need from the shelves, bundling them into Gruff's arms.

"This is a bad idea, Wren," Gruff tells me, I'm ready to snap back with a retort but when I turn to Ryker I notice how very nervous he is. Shit, now my guilt is warring with the anxiety inside of me.

"It's fine, let's just get this and we can go."

"You don't need anything else?"

I grab some heat pads and a packet of painkillers and then shake my head, "This'll be fine, let's go."

He sighs with relief and we begin to make our way back down the aisle. A familiar face right at the end catches my attention.

"Shit," I hiss, grabbing Ryker and tugging him down another aisle, hiding.

"What!?" He hisses.

"I know him," I point to the familiar face at the end of the aisle. Griff, my personal trainer and self-defense teacher. Once upon a time I would have never questioned whether I trusted him but it's obvious that Valentine has had a lot of influence on my life if Lex is telling the truth. I still needed to learn it all but I knew enough.

Was it Lawson or Valentine forcing me into that training? Either way, neither of them could be trusted. Who was Griff really?

I used to trust this man without question but now as I look at him, I realize he's just like the rest. There's a darkness I hadn't recognized before, a way he holds himself, a controlled beast that when rattled will be unleashed.

"Who is it?" Ryker asks.

"His name is Griffin, I used to train with him."

"Okay, so what?"

"He was employed by my father."

"Which one?"

I roll my eyes, "Lawson."

"Who was likely instructed by Valentine."

I nod my agreement. I hated this. I hated that I didn't know what was real and what wasn't, who I could trust and who I couldn't.

He did this to me. Alexander Silver.

My life would have been fine had he never showed up.

But would I really want to go on without knowing him if I knew what I know now?

That was a question for another time.

Griff loiters at the end of the aisle, perusing the shelves and I spot a second man close by, a big guy and he's cornering a smaller man. Shit.

"We need to get out of here," Ryker says.

"No shit."

"Just dump the stuff," I say, "we'll come back later."

"No we take it," Ryker growls, "we ain't coming back out."

I'm sure if the moment required it, Gruff would use his weapons but I hoped it wouldn't come to that.

Gruff guides me the opposite way down the aisle, away from Griffin, Ryker still clutching the haul of womanly products with bright pink and purple packaging in his arms. If nerves and adrenaline weren't causing chaos inside me I'd laugh at the situation.

We slip down an aisle a couple of rows down that would bring us out directly in front of the doors and make a beeline for it, that is until Griffin steps out in front of us.

His eyes are trained on me, hard and yet soft all the same.

"Wren," his eyes dart to the left just as Ryker shuffles the stuff in his hands to one side and reaches for his gun. I still his movements, hoping like hell it isn't a mistake.

"Griffin," I greet.

His eyes bounce between me and Ryker, calculating, trying to figure out what this is. I'm sure he's heard about Lex and me and everyone knows the man next to me is not Lex.

Griffin turns his attention back to me, scanning from the top of my head to the tips of my feet, "Are you okay?"

I frown but nod, "I am."

"They told me Silver took you, kidnapped and hurt you."

I knock my head side to side, "Some of that is true but I'm fine."

"What bits?" He growls.

I have no idea what the fuck is going on here, "It doesn't matter."

"You're not safe Wren," Griff says, looking to Ryker and then back at me.

"From whom?"

"Anyone."

Tears sting my eyes.

"You need to get out of here." Griffin steps closer, his brows drawn down low.

"Stop," Ryker growls, positioning himself in front of me.

"I won't hurt her."

"Like Lawson wouldn't?" Ryker snaps.

"I heard about that, I was told it wasn't true but it is? Lawson tried to kill you?"

"He did," I confirm.

Griff drops his head and takes a deep breath before seeming to come to a decision. He holds one hand out to Ryker and then gestures to his pocket, "I'm just getting a piece of paper and a pen."

Ryker grunts but nods and we both watch Griff reach

into the inside of his jacket, to his pocket where he pulls
out a small notebook and a silver pen. He rips out a
piece of paper and then writes something on it.

Ryker shoves me harder behind his body when Griffin
takes a step closer and hands us over the piece of paper.
Ryker takes it but I see it quickly before he stuffs it into
his pocket. A phone number.

"Remember what I taught you," Griffin says, "Use it
and trust no one." His eyes bounce to Ryker again before
landing on me. "Stay safe Wren, stay alive."

27

Lex

No matter which way I look, there's an enemy.

A fucker trying to take my kingdom, to take what belongs to me. I have them both for the time being, both Wren and the city but with all this new information I wonder if I can keep them both.

It's not gone unnoticed how distracted I've been. Whilst my men don't outright say it – they would be stupid to – they look at me as if I'm walking a fine line of completely losing it.

Exhaustion tugs at me as I make the final few steps up to the mansion and when I touch the handle I can't help but feel some sort of sense of foreboding. I stare down at my white shirt that's not so white anymore, instead it's splattered with blood and dirt. I would have usually had Ryker with me today but truth was I couldn't trust anyone anymore.

I have a mole. In my fucking ranks, I have a fucking mole.

They've been feeding shit back to Valentine and the Syndicate the entire time. My plans, business dealings, fuck even how often I've been alone with Valentine's precious daughter.

He wants her back. Bad.

But something still doesn't sit right.

He abandoned her. Left her to be raised by someone else, that doesn't tell me he's a man who cares for her. He wants her for something else. I thought it was to take over the family business but I no longer believe that.

There's a lot I've learned about Valentine and everything tells me he wouldn't want a woman ruling his legacy. He's misogynistic, cruel with women and bigoted. He wants her for something else. Something big if he's ignoring the directions the Syndicate are giving him.

But what?

I open the door quietly, stepping into the foyer. Raised voices coming from the kitchen tell me that's where Wren and Ryker are.

"Just call it!" Wren yells, frustrated.

"We need to wait for Lex!" Ryker growls back with enough anger to make my blood boil. Friend or not, that's my woman. Mine. And no one speaks to her like that.

I shut the door quietly, despite wanting to barge in there and knock his teeth out for speaking to her that way.

"Why?" Wren sighs, "just call it! He didn't give it to

you anyway!"

I step quietly through the hall, stopping at the threshold but keeping myself concealed around the corner.

"Just wait, Wren."

"Wait for what?" My voice startles my little bird enough for her to jump in her seat. She spins around to face me, her wide green eyes first looking at my face and then the state of my clothes. Granted, this isn't the best way for her to see me, but it is who I am. She's a part of it now, whether she likes it or not.

"Lex," Ryker sighs heavily.

"What are we waiting for?"

"Ryker and I took a little trip today."

The news hits me like a truck to the body. He let her out the house! He knows how unsafe it is for her right now. My anger boils and my blood fizzes in my veins, furious and unrelenting.

"You took her out!?" I bellow. "Are you fucking stupid!?" I should get answers. I should find out why but all I see is red. He put her in danger. He took her out of this house. He could have got her killed or kidnapped. Fuck. I fly across the kitchen, my knuckles meeting his face like a rock to the skull. His head snaps to the side as blood sprays from his mouth.

"Lex!" Wren's voice is muffled to the rage booming inside my ears.

My fist connects with his cheekbone, and I raise my fist to hit him again but he manages to dodge this one, getting in his own hit. I spit blood onto the kitchen tiles, before taking another hit.

"Fuck you, Lex!" Ryker bellows.

"Enough!" Wren screams, scrambling her small body across the kitchen island before stumbling off of it to stand between us. If either of us want to go at each other again we'd have to go through her. She glares at me, squaring her shoulders in front of Ryker as if protecting him.

Jealously hits me hot and heavy, punching me straight in the gut.

"It's not his fault, I made him."

I scoff, "You're no taller than five three little bird and weigh what, a hundred and twenty pounds soaking wet, you're telling me you *made* him."

She rolls her eyes, "Don't be a sexist pig!" she snaps. There's so much fire in her eyes, so much heat warring with anger, "I will hit you."

"And I'll like it," I growl back.

"You two are fucked up," Ryker huffs, collapsing down into the chair, wiping his mouth on the sleeve of his jacket.

My hands shake with the unleashed anger but when Wren steps forward, no less angry and presses her palm to the centre of my chest, over the dried blood and against my rampaging heartbeat it sizzles. I stare down at her, nostrils flaring, trying to keep hold of those last remaining scraps of my anger. Anger is easy. You understand it.

This fucking feeling in my chest, this is not easy.

This is a complication. A mess. A distraction.

But I still raise my hand and place it over hers as I drag her closer with my other one. I press my lips to hers, a contrast to the war in my body and she kisses me back.

I'm in so much fucking trouble with this woman. So much so I'm not sure either of us are going to come out of this alive.

Wren

I feel his tension building in his muscles, the anger rolling off him in waves that send shivers down my spine. His knuckles are split, blood splattered across his skin. I guess that now matches the rest of him. His white shirt is speckled in rust coloured spots and I have no doubt his jacket and pants would be too, I just can't see it because they're black.

Why doesn't that repulse me?

I slip my fingers between two of his shirt buttons, feeling the searing heat of his skin against the pads of my fingers. His heartbeat is steady and strong, pulsing under my touch. He looks down at me, hoods of his eyes lowered, the silver of his eyes glowing.

Slowly, so very slowly, the corners of his mouth tip up in a resemblance of a smile. One brow cocks and he leans in, his breath whispering against my skin as his lips brush against the lobe of my ear.

"Did you miss me little bird?" He whispers so only I can hear.

Ryker is still grumbling behind me but in this moment we're alone, just him and me. Tingles run through my body chaotically, warming me, or perhaps they're warning me.

My nails bite into the firm skin on his chest and he retaliates by nipping my ear, scraping his teeth across the skin. Before I can lose myself in him, before I can forget everything I know is right, he pulls away and levels me with a look that tells me he is less than impressed.

"Where did you go today, little bird?"

"The store," I shrug pulling my hand back and curling my fingers into the palm of my hand.

"And what did you need at the store that someone else couldn't have gotten you? Do you understand how much danger you're currently in?"

He's speaking to me like I'm a child. And it annoys the shit out of me.

"Danger *you* put me in," I retort.

His eyes narrow, "Don't push me right now."

I scoff, "I had to go to the store seeing as I am female

and females tend to have cycles. I required products to stop me bleeding all over your pretty furniture."

"That doesn't explain why someone else couldn't have gone."

I laugh out loud, the sound so violent in the quiet of the kitchen that I make myself jump, "Oh I'm sorry, your right hand over here can shoot people and torture them but he can't seem to go out and buy feminine products without turning green."

Lex's lips twitch as he fights his smile. He looks over my head to Ryker and I turn around, seeing him shrug. Pathetic.

"So what are you waiting for?" He presses.

I sigh. I wanted to phone Griffin the moment we got back to the house but Ryker wouldn't give me his phone or the number. Granted, I saw his reasoning but still, I was getting fed up being told what to do.

"I saw someone today, someone I used to be friends with. He told me to contact him if we wanted more information."

"It's a trap." Lex grunts.

"You're all very paranoid, you know that?" I cock a hand on my hip. "I trust Griffin." Kind of.

"Griffin?" Lex's eyes pin me in place.

Oh boy. Here we go.

28

Lex

Jealousy isn't something I've had a lot of experience with. There isn't much I don't have or don't get, I've never needed to be envious. I know what it looks like, I've seen it in action but this feeling in my body, it's wild and frantic. My heart beats hard, my scalp tingles and my stomach churns, all at the prospect of another man being in Wren's life.

One she so called *trusts*.

Trust is a fickle beast, once you give it someone they have the power over you. They can break you. Betray you. Kill you. And you're blind to it because of so called trust.

There's very few people I trust. I can count on one hand who they are and that's only because they have proven themselves.

Wren doesn't understand.

She trusts blindly. Freely. But she doesn't understand

the repercussions of misplaced trust, especially when involved in this life.

Griffin is from her old life, one connected to Valentine and if there is anything I have learned about that man and his men, all of them and I mean *all* of them are snakes.

I see the moment Wren decides to fight back. I've started to learn a lot about this woman, her tells, her triggers, and with her spine straightening and the rims of her nostrils flaring I know she's about to spit venom.

"Don't you dare," she seethes.

I smirk, the jealousy settling a little, "Don't what, little bird?"

"This," she waves her hand around, "This whole jealousy thing. You don't get to be jealous, asshole. I've known Griffin for years. *Years.* I trust him."

"Like you trusted Lawson?"

Her head snaps back and she strikes, her hand slapping across my face. The sting is sharp, tingles rushing over my cheek and jawline. Slowly I bring my head back, staring down at her. Ryker stands to intervene but I subtly shake my head as I step forward.

"Don't push me, Wren," I growl.

She does just that. She throws her entire body weight at me, trying to force me away but her slight frame is nothing on mine. I grab her, hauling her to my chest before I press her against the nearest counter, pinning her arms in place.

She thrashes around but ultimately, she can't escape me. She'll never be able to.

"You're a fucking asshole. I hate you!"

"Whether you like it or not," she struggles and I have to readjust to keep her in place, "you're a part of this now. You have to question everything and everyone. Lawson raised you, he fucking raised you and he tried to kill you!"

"It's your fault!"

It was. That was true.

But there was nothing to do about that now.

"Regardless, Wren, anyone and I mean *anyone* from your previous life, they don't exist anymore. All you have are enemies."

"And you? Are you my enemy?" She cries.

"No, little bird, I'm not your enemy."

"Then what?" She laughs manically, tears rolling down her face. I'm not entirely sure she even realizes she's crying but her lips wobble and her eyes glaze and something twists inside me. Like the blade of a knife being stabbed into my abdomen and then being twisted. "You're my knight in shining armour? You're here to save the day and we can live happily ever after!?"

Ryker quietly steps from the table, our earlier confrontation forgotten as he nurses his swollen lip and split brow. He looks at me with a mixture of shock and concern? He surely can't think this little thing could do me any damage. But then hell hath no fury than a woman scorned.

"I'm not that either," I say eventually now we are alone.

"Then what, Alexander Silver? What are you if not my enemy?"

"Just yours."

Her eyes widen, the tears still spilling down her rosy cheeks.

"W-what?"

Slowly, I begin to loosen my grip on her, raising my hand as if I'm placating a terrified animal. I tip her chin back, forcing her to level her stare with mine.

"You belong to me Wren, you are *mine*. But where you are mine, I am yours. This is a two way street."

"You act as if people are things to possess."

"Are they not?"

She shakes her head.

I stroke my thumb across her plump bottom lip, grinning at the full body shiver it elicits, "Whether you like it or not, we are one. I'll never let you go. We rule together and those enemies, they are my enemies and we take them down. Together."

"This isn't war, Lex."

"Oh but that's where you are wrong little bird, there's always a war."

"But Griffin –"

"Is on your father's payroll," I interrupt, "and therefore cannot be trusted."

She shakes her head and huffs a breath, exasperated. "You need to shower."

She isn't done with the argument, I know she isn't, she just doesn't have an answer right now.

"I do." I step away from her body, waiting and watching, expecting her to flee, when she doesn't, I tip my head, "join me."

She shakes her head.

"That wasn't a request, little bird."

Her eyes narrow and she purses her lips, "and you're going to need to learn to take *no* for an answer."

She spins away from me, slipping from the kitchen. I hear her take the stairs two at a time, bypassing my room to favor the attic bedroom. I'll remedy that later tonight but for now I let her go.

Before I head up to clean up, I go in search of Ryker, finding him hovering in the living room, nursing a scotch and an ice pack.

"I wouldn't have let anything happen to her," he tells me, spotting me in the threshold.

"This Griffin, what did you think?"

Ryker frowns, "I didn't get much of an impression, you want to contact him?"

I nod once, "contact him from a burner. Set it up. Somewhere public. I want him to come alone."

"The club?"

"Do it in a few days. There's a couple of leads I want to follow before I contemplate using one of Valentine's men."

"He could have taken her out you know," Ryker tells me, "he wasn't alone, I spotted at least four others with him, he let her go."

"A false sense of security is what will get you killed, old friend."

He winces, "yes, boss."

I leave him with my instruction and head up, unbuttoning my shirt as I go. The blood on the shirt has seeped through, leaving faint red splotches on my skin.

Another dead end lead. Ainsley had given me names. Names of people supposedly linked to the Syndicate only they had fuck all for me, either that or they were more terrified of them than they were of me. And that was going to be a big problem.

I was still no closer to figuring out who they were and Valentine was only getting more persistent in his plots to get his daughter back.

Wren doesn't think this is a war, but this is going to be the bloodiest battle this city has ever seen.

And me, the twisted fuck that I am, was going to paint the streets red with their blood and stand atop the pile of bodies of those who dare question me.

The Syndicate may think they have me cornered, trapped with no way out and Valentine can believe all he likes that he has some hope of getting Wren back but if I am nothing else, I am resilient.

They can push and they can pull, but there was no way in this hell or the next I was giving up what belonged to me.

29

Lex

I head up to the attic bedroom after showering, finding
Wren curled up in the centre of the bed. Her breathing is
even and steady so I cross the room, looking down at
her. She's curled on her side, hands beneath her face
with her wild hair stretched across the pillow like
flames.

I lean down and scoop my arms under her body. She
groans but lets me lift her, cradling her to my chest as I
leave the room and head back to the master bedroom.

"I can sleep alone," she mumbles sleepily, nuzzling her
face into my chest.

"That's not how this works," I whisper back, kicking
the door open and then placing her into the queen sized
bed in my bedroom. She doesn't get up and leave,
instead, she scoots herself into the middle and buries
herself under the blankets, one eye watching me over the
sheets.

I flick the switch and climb in beside her, pulling her
closer, wrapping my arms around her. She sighs heavily

and begins to circle her forefinger on my chest.

"You should not have left the compound," I say after a beat of silence.

"You can't keep me locked away forever."

"I can," I tell her, "do not forget who you are dealing with little bird."

"Like I could forget, Lex," she huffs, trying to pull away from me.

I don't let her go, not even an inch. "You belong to me and there are people out there who want to take you away."

"You make this hard," she answers. Life with me, it was never going to be easy for her. But she'd get used to it. And she'll learn her place.

We lay in silence until her breathing steadies back out and she relaxes against me, finally asleep again.

I don't sleep though. I lay there, staring up at the darkened ceiling with her in my arms.

Everything in me that feels for her seems too big, too strong, too fierce, forget just Valentine and the Syndicate, I'm sure I'd take the entire fucking world on if it meant her staying right where she is now.

It's become more than revenge. More than the city.

I'd never thought about taking a wife. Or I had, but in the sense of continuing my lineage but nothing more, with her though, I want it all. I want the marriage and the children with my surname and her fire. I wanted her to stand by my side with our enemies slain and the city at our feet.

On the bedside table my phone buzzes loudly against the top, the vibrations shaking the frame. I quickly reach out and snatch it off, glancing at the name lighting up the screen. My brows pull down. Ainsley didn't phone me. She phoned Ryker.

Gently, I pry Wren from my body and answer the phone, not saying a word until I'm out of the bedroom.

"Ainsley." I greet.

"I'm fucked."

The second floor of the house is dark but I know my men are around here somewhere. I don't go looking for them, instead I take the stairs and head to the office, settling in the chair behind the desk that's been in my family for generations.

"What's going on?" I ask.

"I did something, Lex," she breathes heavy down the line as if she's jogging. The sound of her feet setting a steady rhythm joins the sound of her ragged breath. "They're coming for me."

"Who?"

"The Syndicate."

My spine straightens as my hand curls into a fist atop the desk, "What did you do, Ains?"

"I need to get to you," Ainsley says to me, "But not now, they'll be expecting it. I have shit you can use,

Lex. I have it all."

"Ainsley, how do you know they're coming?"

She laughs but it lacks humour, "I got the message loud and clear."

"Where are you going?" I slam a fist down, "We can protect you."

"No, you can't. Don't underestimate them, Lex, they are bigger than any of us could have expected. They have *everything*. Valentine is a pawn to them. Nothing more. They don't like getting their hands dirty but trust me, if they have to, they will."

"What did you get?"

"Everything Lex, all of it. I can't, not on the phone, when I can, I'll be back."

"And Ryker?"

"Tell him for me?"

"Do I look like your errand boy?"

She laughs, "You're an asshole. Please, tell him."

I sigh.

Ainsley wasn't supposed to be a part of this crew. She didn't fit. But I took her in anyway, thanks to whatever obsession Ryker has with her, and since then she's become as important as Ryker. A sister in arms.

"Sure. Stay safe, get me that information,"

"Yes, boss."

She hangs up. I try the line again a few minutes later and all I get is a disconnection message. Good girl.

If she's right and the syndicate are big enough to scare her off when she knows she has an army at her back then clearly I am underestimating their power. I dial Ryker and relay her message before hanging up to Ryker cussing up a storm.

Ainsley is smart. She's a fighter. She can hold her own until I figure this shit out.

I'm still waiting on my father to give me what he knows but he's been ignoring my calls which tells me there's shit he's sitting on and keeping me in the dark.

And that pisses me off.

With no more to it, I head back up to Wren, finding her still in the same position I left her in. I have no hope of sleeping but I can hold her at least.

She's an antidote to calm the beast inside me. She pushes me, tests me, infuriates me but I always have a leash. One she has wrapped around her hand, holding me tight. With her, I don't worry about losing my shit, I don't worry about going too far. In a world where everyone bends to me it's nice to have someone to disobey me and test my boundaries.

With her warmth enveloping me like a blanket, I push further into the bed.

All this shit isn't going anywhere, it'll be here tomorrow so I take tonight. I take the peace and the warm body next to me, and I'll keep taking until it's ripped from bloody and broken body.

"You called him!?" Wren seethes.

Ryker sighs heavily.

It's been four days since Ainsley ran and Ryker contacted Griffin.

"Yes, Wren, I called him," Ryker confirms.

She purses her lips and glares at him, "Why didn't you let me do it? I doubt he was all that happy hearing from you."

"Because you're naïve!" Ryker snaps.

I shoot him a look to tell him to rein it in and whilst he doesn't like it, he nods subtly. "Look, Wren, we've been doing this a lot longer than you have, there are ways to deal with this shit."

Ryker turns back to me, sighing heavily, rubbing his temples. "Tonight. Eleven PM at the club."

"I'm coming!" Wren declares.

"No," both Ryker and I say at the same time.

"You can't keep me in the dark!" she snaps, "if you

want me to be a part of this shit then I need to know. It would be good to understand what is coming after me. I'm a big girl, I can take care of myself and I need to be prepared."

I narrow my eyes, taking in the stubborn set of her jaw, the way she's begging with her eyes but her mouth stays flat and angry.

Fuck.

This fucking woman. She's going to be the death of me.

"Fine." I growl.

"What!?" Both Ryker and Wren say in unison.

"You can come but you do not leave my side, do you understand me?"

"Yes."

"Lex, you can't be serious, she's a liability."

"Watch your mouth."

"Boss, come on."

"Protect her at all costs. Get several men together, I want them all over the club, on the door, in the fucking bathrooms. I want every single person searched before they come in, no exceptions. Do it now. Get it sorted."

With a sigh, Ryker dips his chin and leaves Wren and me in the kitchen. She curls her hands around her mug and grins, satisfied with her win.

"Don't test me, Wren. I'm allowing this because you

have history but if he so much as looks at you wrong, I will end him."

"Understood."

"Good girl."

She tries to hide the small smile my words elicit and the blush that creeps up her cheeks makes my dick hard.

I've seen just how far that blush goes.

Cocking my head to the side, I watch her, the way she pulls her hair over one shoulder, her eyes looking at everything but me. Her teeth tug at her bottom lip.

"Little bird," I coo.

Her eyes rise to meet mine as I begin to unbutton my shirt.

"I'm going to shower. Join me."

I don't wait for an answer and my mouth tugs up when I hear her slip from her stool and follow after me.

She was mine. She knew it. I knew it.

I was never letting her go.

30

Wren

I watch his back as he climbs the stairs and then follow his body down the long hallway to the master bedroom where he proceeds to strip from his shirt.

I follow the lines of his well toned muscle, watching it flex and roll with all the lethal grace of a cat. The light catches the silver lines of scars that mark his skin but it adds to his brutal beauty. He doesn't once look back at me as he heads into the bathroom where he proceeds to turn the shower on.

I wait until I hear the door to the shower open and then I strip from my clothes and head through to the bathroom naked. He stands beneath the cascading spray with one arm outstretched, palm resting on the tiles and his head tilted down so the water hits the back of his neck.

I climb in behind him, running a hand up his spine, watching the muscles jump under my touch.

I had fallen in love with a monster.

A twisted king.

When you can't run from the monsters, you join them. You stand at their side and watch the world burn all around you.

My fingers trace the lines of his scars before whispering up to the bumps of his ribcage and following the curve until I can flatten my palm over his left pec, his heart beat a steady thump under my hand.

His body visibly shivers under my touch.

He's a glorious work of art, every single inch, all the way down to his blackened soul.

Leaning forward, I press my lips to his shoulder blade, the skin wet and slick under my mouth.

"Little bird," he rasps.

"Touch me," I beg.

Slowly he turns in the shower and grips my hips, eyes devouring every inch of my naked skin. His hands skirt up my belly, over my naval, following the curves of my body until he cups my breasts, fingers pinching my nipples, twisting them until it boarders the threshold between pleasure and pain.

When my mouth opens on a gasp he captures the sound with his lips, his tongue plunging in to duel with mine.

Desire shoots through me, the blood rushing to my core fast enough to make my thighs tingle and pussy clench.

My hair is slick and sticking to my back and my mouth is swollen from his rough kisses when he drops to his knees, hooks one of my legs over his shoulder and presses his tongue to my clit, expertly flicking it with the tip in a way that makes my knees buckle. He alternates between teasing kisses and rough devouring, sucking the sensitive flesh into his mouth until I'm grinding against his face, begging for mercy. Begging for the release that keeps me constantly on the edge, teetering ever closer to the vertical drop that promises a world of pleasure and pain. When he inserts two fingers into me, I shatter. My cries echo off the walls, vibrating the glass panels that enclose us in the shower and when I don't think I can take anymore, he curls his fingers in my channel and draws another from my body, leaving me shaking uncontrollably. Slowly, pressing kisses up my stomach and breasts, he rises to his full height, pressing a teasing kiss to my lips before he roughly spins me and forces my hands out, pressing my palms to the tiles.

He kicks my legs out, separating them and lines his cock with my entrance.

"I dream of your pussy, little bird," he growls, the head of his dick nudging me open.

I groan at the filth leaving his mouth but the sound gets trapped in my throat as he pistons forward and spears me on is cock. He presses into my spine, forcing it to curve more so my ass juts out and with one hand holding me in position and the other gripping my hip hard enough to bruise he pulses his hips, pushing in deeper with each thrust.

He rolls his hips, slowing his movements, fingers kneading my flesh as he dips his knees and pushes in further, the head of his cock rubbing against the sweet spot inside me.

My eyes roll back in my head as he rides off the back of my previous orgasms, pulling my body tight, too tight, it'll snap.

"Yes, Lex," I moan, "Oh fuck."

"Tell me," he rasps.

"I'm yours," I need no prompting.

His hand slips up my spine as he fists my wet hair into his hand, curling the strands between his fingers near the root and tugging, pulling my head back so my throat curves. I boarder a very thin line, the biting sting of my hair being pulled only adding to the intensity building inside of me.

His fingers curl tighter, my scalp biting as his hips drive into me, over and over again, our wet skin slapping together obscenely loud.

"You're mine," he bellows, "only mine. *Always* mine."

"Yes!" my voice is strained as stars begin to explode behind my eyes.

"Come for me, little bird." He growls. "I want to feel you come all over my cock."

He pushes in so hard I feel my bones rattle and then I'm coming. No I'm flying. My whole body pulls tight and then… it releases.

My scream bounces back at me, my heart feels as if it's pounding straight through the wall of my chest, battering against my ribcage almost painfully but the climax continues to cause chaos through my body. My muscles spasm, my walls clench and my toes curls.

Lex grunts and roars behind me, his thrusts becoming spontaneous but no less hard as he releases inside me. I feel him fill me up, my walls drawing every last drop from him.

His hand gently releases my hair and I drop my head forward, stretching out the taut muscles in the back of my neck. He's still holding my hips, his cock still buried deep inside me as he leans over me and presses the most tender of kisses to my spine, a complete contrast to the ruin he just caused.

Softly, he bands an arm around my waist and raises me to a standing position, his shaft slipping from my body as he presses my back to his chest. He reaches down and lifts a sponge and some soap, pouring the creamy liquid onto the surface and then sliding it over my pale skin. The soap is cold against my heated flesh but it feels so good. Goosebumps chase of my skin as he lathers it over my body, over the mounds of my breasts, across the tight line of my stomach. He moves my hair out of the way to get to my collar bones and throat, working the sponge over my sensitive flesh.

I don't stop him when he spins me and drops to a crouch, running the sponge over my thighs and then dips it between my legs. I jump when he presses the softness to my centre, washing away the evidence of him on my skin.

He tends to me like I'm the most precious thing in the world to him. Like I am a rare gem and should he take his eye off me for just a moment, I'll disappear.

The same hands that have killed, tortured, maimed are the ones working through my hair. He tips my head beneath the spray, wetting it further. He then squirts shampoo into the tresses.

"What are you doing?" I whisper.

"Loving you," he answers easily, his fingers working through the strands to bring it to a lather.

My eyes roll to the back of my head with each press of his fingers to my scalp.

I let him *love* me.

I let the nightmare that is Alexander Silver care for me.

31

Lex

Wren steps out of the attic bedroom, closing the door softly behind her.

"You look stunning," I tell her, eyes raking over the length of her. She's in a black silk dress with thin straps and a low neckline, the material teases her frame without being too tight and sits mid-thigh, giving me a good view of her creamy thighs. Her feet are strapped up in a pair of heels and she's pulled all her hair to sit across one shoulder, the tresses wild with curls that bounce on the mounds of her breasts.

Her eyes meet mine before dropping to my lips and then the rest of me.

We needed to make it look completely normal for our meeting with Griffin. If we turned up ready for war people would cotton on to the fact that we have an outsider in our midst, so I'm dressed in a charcoal grey tailored suit, the white shirt is unbuttoned at the top and I've buttoned the jacket. My hands are buried in my pockets but my hands twitch to touch her skin, to feel her softness beneath my fingers.

I take her arm when we reach the bottom of the stairs and head out into the unseasonably chilly night. Clouds cover the darkened sky, the moon suffocated beneath the thick blanket and a wind disturbs the oaks that line the property. Wren slides into the back of the SUV and I follow, pulling her back to me when she tries to sit on the other side.

She shakes her head but settles into my side anyway.

The gravel in the drive crunches beneath the tires as we begin to make our way down the long road.

My hand lazily draws circles on her bare shoulder, "I want you to be careful tonight." I tell her.

"I'll be fine," she sighs.

I can't help but feel like that's a lie. Not an intentional one but the sense of foreboding weighs on me heavily.

It's a set up.

An ambush.

Now that I have Wren, I couldn't bear to part with her. She was a drug and like all addicts I needed her more and more each day.

Was I selfish? Of course I was.

I knew keeping her with me was doing more harm than good, but the threat is there now, I can't simply hand her back. Marcus Valentine wants her for something, and I know it isn't to continue his fucked up legacy and the Syndicate have now made attempts on her life twice.

Both times being when she was with me.

I was losing control.

I couldn't let that happen.

Heading out tonight wasn't only for informative purposes, it proves to all the fuckers baring down on us that we are resilient. We won't be suppressed. We don't fear them.

This has been my city for a long time and the Silver's for longer than any of them have probably been alive. To get the key they'd have to pry it from my cold dead fingers.

"Little bird," I tip up her chin, "I know you will be, but I mean it, nonetheless, do not leave my side."

"As if you'd let me," she scoffs with a tease.

I push my thumb between her lips, suppressing a groan when she wraps her plump lips around the digit and sucks. "This mouth will get you into trouble." I warn.

She cocks a brow in challenge, "Will it get me into trouble, or you?"

I laugh, oh that mouth could get me into a lot of trouble. Her teeth graze over the skin on my finger before she releases it and leans forward to kiss my throat. When she pulls back her brows are drawn low, her eyes searching my face as if she's looking for answers to questions in her head.

"What is it?" I ask.

She shakes her head, glancing away, "nothing."

She's lying.

"Come, little bird," I pull her back, "what is going inside that head?"

"We're here," the driver interrupts, giving Wren the perfect opportunity to slip from my grasp and head out the door being held open for her on the other side of the car. My guy stands close, using his body to shield hers as ordered.

Did Valentine or even the Syndicate have this type of loyalty? To protect a woman even if that meant using your own body to shield her from any oncoming attacks? I doubted it.

He shows her to the door, me following close behind as we slip in. Ryker will already be here somewhere, and Griffin should be arriving in a little over an hour.

We head through the lower section of the club, weaving through the figureheads letting off steam where no watchful eyes can judge their actions.

"This city is truly corrupt," Wren comments when we step into the elevator that'll take us to the balcony. It's been repaired since the attack, the glass now reinforced incase that kind of incident were to happen again. It appeared the Syndicate didn't care whether or not this war was kept private, they are not directly linked and therefore cannot be accused. They sit in their comfy chairs in their offices, watching the mess they've created.

They believe themselves to be Gods.

We'll prove just how wrong they are.

"There's a little darkness in everyone," I say as the doors slide closed.

"Do you not feel guilty for this?" She asks with a frown.

"If it isn't us, then it'll be someone else," I tell her honestly, "we've controlled this city and the underground for hundreds of years, long before either of us were even born. The Silver's keep the streets clean."

She laughs without humor, "Hardly clean, Lex, you traffic drugs, guns, money."

"We do," I confirm, "but I personally don't do that, I just control those who do. If it weren't me then the drugs on our streets would be worse and dirty, the gun violence ten times worse than it already is. Gangs and pimps and dealers would rule here, we ensure that doesn't happen."

"You personally don't do that, but you'll kill someone."

"To those who deserve it, yes."

"And Valentine?"

"Valentine is a parasite, little bird, a small fish swimming with sharks. He believes he's capable of taking this city."

"So it's just a power trip?"

"No, he killed my mother. You were my vengeance until…"

"I became your pawn." She finishes.

"You're more than that now."

She sighs heavily, "You'll kill him?"

"Eventually but right now, I have bigger problems to deal with."

"Like?"

"The Syndicate."

She shakes her head, "It's all very political."

I laugh, "Yes."

"And what happens if I don't want any part of this?" She questions after a short silence, "will you let me go?"

"No," my answer is quick and snappy. "You're mine little bird, you'll realize that soon enough."

She doesn't say anymore on the matter as we step onto the balcony. Music thumps through the speakers and the dance floor is filled with bodies gyrating and pulsing to the music. The incident from a few weeks ago forgotten.

The stench of alcohol saturates the air around us but there's a tinge of something else in the air. Something metallic and stifling though I can't place it.

Ryker is lounging on the couch, a scotch in a small tumbler held between his fingers and resting on his knee. He's pinching the bridge of his nose, eyes squeezed shut.

We haven't heard a peep from Ainsley since she went into hiding. Ryker is frantic but it pushes this shit with the Syndicate. We need that information. She will be fine and will keep out of trouble until we can figure this shit out.

"Gruff," Wren plops herself next to my right hand and steals his whiskey, tipping it back before Ryker can stop her. "That's good shit."

"Yeah it is," Ryker growls, "And you just drank it."

I wave a finger to the server and gesture for drinks as I settle into the couch opposite and beckon Wren to my side.

She stares at me, her face telling me all the things her mouth wants to. Basically, fuck you.

"Little bird," I drawl, "What did we talk about in the car?"

She growls but gets up, crossing the short space to throw herself down next to my side. I hook her around the waist and drag her close, holding her to my body.

"Any news?" I ask Ryker.

He shakes his head, "Griffin was spotted about twenty minutes away. They'll let him through the underground."

"Good."

Now we wait.

32

Wren

Lex is tense besides me, he acts cool, collected but his body is coiled tight, like a snake ready to strike, his muscles hard, fingers squeezing the glass tumbler in his hand so hard I worry it may shatter.

He hates this.

The lack of control.

The threats.

This is a man who has had everything and never been questioned, now, it's different. The knots are unravelling and he's frantically trying to tighten them without understanding the whole picture.

I didn't understand any of it, how this world worked, how business is exchanged but I knew this wasn't how it was supposed to go. He was the self-proclaimed king and someone else was threatening to take his crown.

His fingers absentmindedly draw circles on my exposed thigh whilst he nurses his scotch.

"He's here," someone says besides us and both Ryker and Lex sit up straighter, eyes lasering in on the elevator doors.

Griffin.

When the metal doors slide open a few minutes later and I get a look at my old friend, I first feel relief and then that all goes out the window when I get a true glimpse at his face. He looks tired, ill, like he hasn't slept in weeks. His shoulders sag, his skin is pale and he doesn't look like the old friend I used to know.

There's an invisible weight on his shoulders.

"Search him." Lex orders.

Two men descend on Griff, forcing his arms wide and his legs apart as they pull and prod his body, searching for weapons. They withdraw a phone from his pocket and a notepad with a pen but that's all they find.

"You really think I'd bring weapons into the devils lair," Griff growls, "it may be stupid to be here, but I am not a fucking idiot."

"Sit." Lex demands, ignoring his statement.

I try to give him a reassuring smile, but he glances away quickly, unable to maintain eye contact. When he does sit, he finally looks at me and then at the hand still rested on my thigh, "You're with him, now?"

"Griff –"

"Don't speak to her," Lex hisses, "This is between you and me. Say what you have to say and then get the fuck out of my club."

"I'm here to help," Griff growls back.

Lex's muscles become increasingly tighter, like pressure under a lid, too much and he'll explode.

"Then help," Lex's fingers bite into my skin, "before I change my fucking mind."

"This is your fucking fault," Griffin roars, "if you hadn't fucking gone after Wren none of this would have happened. You pissed off the wrong man!"

Lex laughs though it's more manic than humored, "You think Valentine scares me?" He says in a voice so low I'm unsure if Griffin actually hears him, "Valentine is nothing. He has no power, no control. No loyalty," the last part of his sentence is spat.

"It isn't Valentine you should be worried about."

"The Syndicate, it's funny, everyone keeps mentioning this organization like they're the boogey man and yet they can't do the work themselves."

"Marcus got involved with the Syndicate a little over a year ago. They contacted him when he first took a shot at the city, telling him they could help. That they had the resources and the man power where he did not. He signed on the dotted line immediately. Wren here, was never supposed to be a part of this though. After a while, Marcus realized that the Syndicate would always be in control. They had him and his men. They were clever really."

"And so what? The Syndicate want the city?"

"Yes, they want you and your men under their thumb whether they have to kill you or not. Marcus was their way in but that's no longer going to work for them."

"Valentine's an idiot."

"Don't underestimate him," Griff warns, "it's become more now. He is thirsty for power and he'll do just about anything to get it, including using his daughter as a bargaining chip. The Syndicate don't like the way he's running things, it brings too much attention but more than that, he's distracted, deviating from the plan and they are prepared to take out anything and everything that stands in their way. Including Wren. Without her, Marcus has no bargaining chip."

His eyes bounce to me and then back to Lex, swallowing visibly.

"What does he plan to use her for?" Lex asks.

Griff shrugs his shoulders, "Whatever it is, it's against the Syndicate and what they are working towards."

Lex

"Where do your loyalties lie, Griffin?" I settle back on the couch, holding onto the one thing grounding me right now.

I fucking knew there was something more to Valentine's need to get his daughter back.

He frowns when one of the girls working the club offers him a scotch, I nod when he looks to me for approval. Good.

He takes the drink and sips it, seeming to relax a little.

"I asked you a question," I press, "Where are your loyalties?"

With a swallow he looks to Wren and sighs as if he holds the world on his shoulders, "With Wren."

With Wren is with me.

"Why?" I ask.

He chews the side of his lip, his eyes touching every inch of her body and then settling on the hand I have on her thigh. The jealous beast inside me rears its ugly head. I know exactly why. It's obvious in the way he looks at her, with a softness only I'm allowed to look at her with.

She is mine.

"The reason why will get me killed."

"Son of a bitch," Ryker hisses.

"Look," Griffin raises his hands, "I'm not here to start anything, I'm here to keep her alive."

"Griffin," Wren has been quiet this entire time though

she's been less than relaxed. She's nervous, fidgeting under my palm, "I don't want you to get hurt."

She cares for him deeply, hurting him will hurt her so I don't do that. I don't hurt him as much as I want to.

He shakes his head, "You need to fix this," he points at me, "you started this mess, you fix it."

Wren settles her hand on mine to stop me from beating the ever-loving shit out of him.

"I want you to get more information," I say through gritted teeth, "You pretend you're so far up Marcus' ass but you report to me now, do you understand?"

"Ha," Griffin scoffs, "I don't owe you shit."

"Then I have no use for you," I reach into the pocket, my fingers curling around the butt of the Glock I have stashed there. It has a silencer but too many eyes to really get away with it.

"Don't!" Wren grabs me, pleading, begging me.

Griffin isn't scared, he doesn't flinch under my venomous glare. "I will do it but not for you, remember that."

Silence falls between us, the music that thumps through the club pounding through my veins. Wren's hand squeezes mine atop her thigh.

"Please," she whispers in my ear, soft enough that only I hear.

Finally breaking away from the stare down with Griffin, I turn to her, taking in the wide eyes, glistening a little with unshed tears and the nervous way she gnaws on her bottom lip. With the hand not holding her leg, I reach up and gently pry her lip from between her teeth, smoothing my finger over the red, swollen skin to soothe the sting left behind.

"For you, little bird," I whisper against her mouth.

33

Lex

Griffin leaves, slipping back down the way he came. My mind goes over all the information he gave me, Marcus, the Syndicate. There's so many pieces of this puzzle and no image to follow.

"Can we dance?" Wren asks.

I look over to her, "You want to dance?"

She nods slowly and then shrugs, "I just want to relax a little."

I glance down at the dancefloor, at the mass of bodies, writhing and pulsing on the dancefloor. I spot my men, posed like security around the club and then glance at the door, at the three guys there searching bags and bodies before they can enter.

She's safe here.

I tip the remaining dregs of my scotch into my mouth and push up from the couch, taking her hand and gently tugging her up with me.

"You're dancing?" Ryker laughs.

"Shut the fuck up."

I jerk my head for two extra guys to follow us down. Ultimately, I could protect her better than any of these but knowing I have back up helps ease the sense of doom currently taking up residence in my stomach.

I don't scare easily. Fear isn't an emotion I'm used to, it was trained out of me at a young age. I don't get scared, people are scared of me. I was taught that the monster under the bed was myself and the only way to survive in a world like mine was to be the villain.

But Wren Valentine terrifies me.

She questions everything, she turns everything I've learned on its head and replaces it with shit I've never even dreamed about having.

She tells me I'm her nightmare but this little bird has it all wrong.

She's the nightmare.

Her hand is soft in mine, loose but there and I grip tighter as we descend the stairs and sink into the heaving crowd.

Finding a spot close to the back of the club, I pull her in close to my body, her breasts pushed against my chest as my hand slips around to hold her at the base of her spine. I feel the warmth of her skin soaking through the silk of her dress, her fragrance assaulting my senses.

I move against her, pressing further into her welcoming body. She's soft where I'm hard, warm where I'm cold. She's everything I can never be, making her the perfect fit by my side.

My lips tease across hers as we dance and her hands slide up my back, the muscles jumping, welcoming her touch.

With a sea of bodies and lights all around me, all I see is this woman. All I feel is her. She has come in and disrupted my controlled chaos, turning my life into a frenzied blur of images.

She has become my weakness and for that I am doomed.

There's absolute zero chance I'd let her go. I've tasted and I've teased, I've fucked and loved and cared for her and now she is mine.

Not Valentine's. Not Griffin's. Not even the fucking Syndicate's.

Mine.

My cock grows hard between our bodies, the shaft pressing heavily into the soft curve of her stomach. A stomach I'll have swollen and round as soon as possible.

She'll carry my child and she'll carry my name and she'll rule this city by my side.

She's the queen and all these fuckers can bow down to her.

"Lex," she whimpers against my mouth, the taste of cranberries lingering on her lips.

The air conditioning blows overhead, carrying a cool breeze onto our bodies. She captures my lip between her teeth, biting down hard enough to make it bleed and then she licks away the sting, sliding her hand between our bodies to grip my dick through the material of my pants.

I needed her.

I needed her here and now.

With a tug of her hand I lead her towards the offices behind the bar, only for personal use but I own the fucking club. The servers behind the bar pay us no mind as I throw the door open and lock it promptly behind us. The music continues to vibrate the walls, muffled and tinny now we are behind closed doors. The only window in the room rattles with the heavy bass that thumps wildly.

"Little bird, don't you know it's not nice to tease," my voice is a rasp, a husky baritone that forces a shiver from her body.

I revel in her reaction to me, the way her body wields to my touch, to my voice, to my every caress.

Wren steps forward and places a hand on my chest, pushing me back until I feel the chair behind my knees. I fall into it, slouching down until my knees are apart and my torso is curled. I rest my head against the backrest, watching my queen.

She takes a step back, the heel of her shoes clipping against the wood flooring.

"Tell me who *you* belong to," she purrs, lids hooded as she watches me slowly begin to unbutton my shirt.

My lips curl into a smirk, "Only you, little bird."

"Tell me what you want me to do." Her fingers play with the thin strap holding her dress up, pushing it down the curve of her shoulder and then back up whilst her other hand lifts the hem of her dress, bringing it up, up, until it shows the dips in her shapely hips and the thin lacy strap of her underwear.

She's so fucking sexy.

My erection pounds behind the zipper of my pants.

"You wanted to dance, little bird," I palm my cock, squeezing hard, "dance for me."

One side of her mouth tilts up and then she spins, showing me her back and the round curves of her ass. The dress clings to the curve, following the length of her spine and then the globes of her ass cheeks, making my mouth water.

She brings her arms up, lifting the mane of wild copper hair until it piles atop her head in a mass of chaotic curls. There's a sheen to her skin, a thin layer of perspiration that makes her skin glow in the lighting of the office, with only a lamp on in the corner emitting a dim orange light, her skin takes on a creamy, golden hue, dusted with fine, light freckles.

She weaves her body, matching the pace of the music, her hips swaying side to side, the dress creasing and bunching with her movements. Her calf muscles work as she bends her knees and lowers a little, dancing for me.

"Spin around," I rasp, biting the inside of my cheek to stop myself from taking her right now. "I want to see your face."

She does as she's told, slowly turning to face me.

There's a pink blush on her cheeks but it isn't from embarrassment, no, I see the darkness in her eyes, the way the pulse point in her neck batters wildly against her skin, like a butterfly trapped in a jar. If I were to slide my hand up her thigh and swipe my fingers through her folds I'm sure I'd find her wet, needy, ready.

She continues her dance, moving her body for me in a way that hypnotizes me. Her hands come up to the straps, dipping beneath the thin material to pull it away from her shoulders but then she drops them again, her hands following the mounds of her breasts to her ribs and her stomach.

A sudden popping sound echoes in the room, loud enough to drown out the music for a split second.

Wren stills in front of me, her eyes widening and instantly, I'm on alert.

My heart begins to pound in my chest as I scramble up from the chair, crossing the small distance between us and gripping the tops of her arms.

"Wren?" I question, "Wren, what is it!?"

Her eyes bounce between mine, her plump and swollen lips parted and then she tilts her chin, looking down between our bodies. I follow her gaze to where her hands are pressed to her stomach.

Red seeps through her fingers and when she pulls her hands away, I see her palms coated in blood.

No.

Oh fuck no.

With a small, frightful cry, her legs buckle beneath her.

I'm quick to catch her, stopping her delicate frame from hitting the floor.

No, no, this can't happen.

I frantically search the room, spotting the perfect hole in the window where the bullet had come through before settling on a club uniform shirt folded on top of the desk. I grab it, pressing it to the wound pulsing blood in her abdomen.

She sucks in a couple of shaky breaths as I hold the fabric to her skin, trying to stem the bleeding.

"It hurts," her voice is steady, despite the shake in her breath and body, "Lex."

"I know, little bird," I can't think straight. I pat my pockets, looking for my phone.

She was safe. She was supposed to be safe.

I come up empty, my phone nowhere on my body but I need help. The music is too loud for anyone to hear me which means I need to get out of here.

Blood stains the crisp white shirt still half way unbuttoned, Wren's blood smearing across my skin.

This was no way the end for us. We had only just begun.

34

Wren

The pain sears through my system as if it's lava rushing through my veins. My skin wet, sticky, the warm blood running off my skin. All I see is red.

Lex presses the balled up wad of fabric to my stomach, holding it over the hole that pulses blood but I can't focus on anything. The edges of my vision pulse with black and white spots, my head feels light, like I'm in the space before you fall asleep, where you're still conscious but barely.

I feel my body being lowered but that doesn't make sense, wasn't I already led down?

The hard floor presses into my back, putting pressure on the wound in my abdomen. The dizziness is chased away at the blinding pain and I'm not able to stop the scream that barrels from my throat.

Is this what death feels like?

Is this it now? I'll go out in a pool of blood with fire in my veins.

"It's okay, shh," Lex pants, "Just, breathe, okay?"

I've never seen him like this. This is a man who fears nothing and yet I swear that's complete terror in his eyes.

I don't like it. A sense of calm begins to wash through my system as I stare at his face. I suppose seeing his brutal beauty isn't such a bad way to go. With my fingers, I run my hand down the side of his face, frowning at the red streaks now marring his skin.

"You're bleeding," I croak.

He shakes his head and then stands, his feet pounding on the floor. I hear the rattle of the door and then the heavy music sweeps through the room like an angry wind but I don't mind the music.

I can sleep with noise, that doesn't bother me and even if it did, I'm so tired right now. So tired.

If I just close my eyes, I can sleep.

So that's what I do… I sleep.

35

Lex

"No!" I scoop her up from the floor, wincing at how rough I'm handling her but I don't have time to be gentle. She needed a hospital. Now. "Don't you dare close your eyes little bird."

Anger pulses through me like a bull, red hot and furious. She doesn't get to leave me like this.

She doesn't get to fucking leave me.

"Wake up Wren," I shake her, feeling the warm droplets of blood running over my hands. How long has it been? Minutes? Fuck I don't now, it feels like hours.

The crowd in the club continues to pulse wildly to the music. No one turns our way, no one even bats an eye at the man holding a bleeding woman in his arms.

I turn to the door but the crowd is too thick to move through without either dropping Wren or hurting her further.

This is the Syndicate.

They got her.

I turn back and tilt my head to the balcony, seeing Ryker on the couch. He's still nursing a scotch, his head tipped back so he's facing the ceiling.

As if sensing my eyes, he slowly lifts his head and meets my stare through the glass.

It doesn't even take him a second.

He jumps up from the couch and begins to shout orders I can't hear over the music. It would be me doing this, but I can't seem to think, let alone talk.

I look down at Wren's sickly pale face, her eyes fluttering closed again.

"Wake up, baby," I shake her, "Wake up."

I needed to get moving.

I push around the edge of the crowd, forcing my way to the stairs and the only easy way out. Ryker is pounding towards me.

"What the fuck happened?" He goes to touch her and something in me snaps. I snatch her away, curling myself around her body as if to protect her though I know, deep down, it isn't Ryker she needs protection from.

It's me.

I caused this. She's bleeding out in my arms because of what *I* did.

That strange scent hits me half a second before an almighty boom rattles the walls of the club.

Both Ryker and I, with Wren in my arms, are thrown off our feet with the blast, fire instantly erupting. Dazed, with my ears ringing I push onto my elbows, reaching for Wren.

She's face down on the ground, her wild cooper hair spilled around her like a fiery halo.

I feel the heat from the flames, can hear the screams and cries of the crowd and feel the stamp of feet vibrating the floor beneath me as they rush for the exit but my focus isn't on that, it isn't on how the fuck this has happened or who, it's only on her.

Pain pulses through my body at the same pace of my frantic heartbeat. I know I'm bleeding, badly but so is she. A red pool is blooming from beneath her body and red tendrils, like crimson snakes run ribbons over her pale skin, over her legs, arms and shoulders.

"Wren," my voice is raspy, "Wren."

With every single ounce of strength I have, I reach her, gently turning her body until she's laying on her back. Her chest rises and falls, and with ash clinging to her dark lashes, she blinks up at me.

She looks completely broken. Battered.

Bruise's bloom across her pale skin, joining with the crimson that runs rivers over her body.

"You're okay baby."

"L-lex," she stutters, sucking in a wheezing breath.

No, no, "You don't get to leave, remember," I growl, "You belong to me, little bird. I say when you are allowed to leave."

Her lips tip up into a small, pained smile, "I love you."

Those three words end me.

I don't deserve love, especially not from her.

I set out to kill her and I've just done that.

"No," I rise up onto my knees, my body screaming out at me, "No, don't sound like you're saying goodbye."

"It's okay."

"No!" I reach down, pushing her wild hair from her face, "you don't leave!" I grit out.

"Kiss me."

"Little bird," I beg.

I've never begged for a single thing in my life.

"Please."

With the world in chaos around me, I lean down and kiss her, tasting the metallic tinge of blood on my tongue.

When I pull away a sudden whack to my head has me falling away from Wren. My skull explodes with a pain so sharp my vision blackens.

Wren is flat on her back, staring at me as a single tear slips from the corner of her eye, running a clean path through the dust, dirt and blood that clings to her skin.

I try to get up but the fogginess in my head makes my limbs too heavy, too weak to move.

Who the fuck hit me!?

Two legs step up beside Wren's body and through bleary eyes I follow them up to find Marcus Valentine standing over his daughter's body.

"Who the fuck did this!?" He bellows, "What good will she be if she's dead!?"

I hear people scurrying around, but I can't see past him and her, somewhere close by a fire crackles wildly, the heat of the flames making my skin too hot.

"Get the fuck away from her!" I growl, finally able to push up onto my elbows, though it's shaky and weak. When I'm there I roll, catching myself before I hit the ground.

A swift boot to the face has me crashing back down.

Get to Wren. I chant the words over and over as I try to push up again.

I keep my eyes on them, watching as I struggle as Valentine leans down and roughly pulls Wren from the rubble, throwing her around too hard. She ends up limp over his shoulder, blood dripping from her skin, mixing into the dirt that crunches under his feet.

"Burn it all to the ground," Valentine meets my eyes, "let them all burn."

His grin is nothing short of menacing.

There's nothing in his eyes, no soul, only darkness and death.

He's truly sold his soul to the devil.

"It's time my daughter and I become reacquainted."

And with those parting words he turns and leaves, taking Wren with him and I'm helpless to stop him.

To be continued....

TWISTED CITY DUET
BOOK II

RIA WILDE

COMING
DECEMBER
2021

I know! That cliffhanger is something else but I promise Twisted King is coming!
Wren & Lex's conclusion is coming December 2021 (earlier if I can get it ready sooner!)
Thank you so much for reading Little Bird!

THANK YOU!

Writing this story has been an adventure and of course it continues! The next installment of Twisted City is coming real soon but thank you for reading the first part of Wren & Lex's story, I hope you loved it as much as I have loved writing it!

Reviews are a huge help for indie authors like me and I'd really appreciate it if you could leave your feedback! I am so appreciative of all my readers so thank you for picking up this book!

Acknowledgements

Where do I start? Firstly, I want to thank my book bestie, Emma for being the very first person to read Little Bird. You listened to all my rants, crazy ideas and plans and supported me and this journey from the very beginning. This book most definitely wouldn't be where it is today without you! To my beta readers and ARC team, you took a chance on a brand new author and your support has helped push me through some difficult parts in this process, so thank you for helping me and for all your kind words! And finally to you, the readers, there are thousands of books out there to pick from but for some crazy reason you picked this one so THANK YOU!

Happy reading everyone! Ria x

ABOUT THE AUTHOR

Bringing you stories that are dirty, dangerous &
deliciously sinful.
Ria Wilde is an indie author who writes dark & sinful
romance. A lover of all things gritty & dark, the anti-
heroes we all hate to love and of course, the
possessive alpha men. When she isn't writing, you'll
likely find her with her nose in a book or doing her
second love, graphic design!

Printed in Great Britain
by Amazon